ROBYN DONALD

Surrender to Seduction

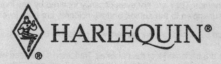

HARLEQUIN®

TORONTO • NEW YORK • LONDON
AMSTERDAM • PARIS • SYDNEY • HAMBURG
STOCKHOLM • ATHENS • TOKYO • MILAN • MADRID
PRAGUE • WARSAW • BUDAPEST • AUCKLAND

If you purchased this book without a cover you should be aware
that this book is stolen property. It was reported as "unsold and
destroyed" to the publisher, and neither the author nor the
publisher has received any payment for this "stripped book."

ISBN 0-373-18707-6

SURRENDER TO SEDUCTION

First North American Publication 1999.

Copyright © 1998 by Robyn Donald.

All rights reserved. Except for use in any review, the reproduction or
utilization of this work in whole or in part in any form by any electronic,
mechanical or other means, now known or hereafter invented, including
xerography, photocopying and recording, or in any information storage
or retrieval system, is forbidden without the written permission of the
publisher, Harlequin Enterprises Limited, 225 Duncan Mill Road,
Don Mills, Ontario, Canada M3B 3K9.

All characters in this book have no existence outside the imagination of
the author and have no relation whatsoever to anyone bearing the same
name or names. They are not even distantly inspired by any individual
known or unknown to the author, and all incidents are pure invention.

This edition published by arrangement with Harlequin Books S.A.

® and TM are trademarks of the publisher. Trademarks indicated with
® are registered in the United States Patent and Trademark Office, the
Canadian Trade Marks Office and in other countries.

Look us up on-line at: http://www.romance.net

Printed in U.S.A.

CHAPTER ONE

GERRY DACRE realised that she'd actually heard the noise a couple of times before noticing it. Sitting on her bed to comb wet black hair off her face, she remembered that the same funny little bleat had teased her ears just before she showered, and again as she came back down the hall.

Frowning, she got to her feet and walked across to the window, pushing open the curtains. Although it was after seven the street-lamps were still struggling against a reluctant New Zealand dawn; peering through their wan light, she made out a parcel on the wet grass just inside the Cape Honeysuckle hedge.

The cry came again, and to her horror she saw movement in the parcel—a weak fluttering against the sombre green wall of the hedge.

'Kittens!' she exploded, long legs carrying her swiftly towards the front door.

Or a puppy. It didn't sound like kittens. How dared anyone abandon animals in her garden—anywhere! Anger tightened her soft mouth, blazed from her dark blue-green eyes as she ran across the verandah and down the wooden steps, across the sodden lawn to the parcel.

It wasn't kittens. Or a puppy. Wailing feebly from a shabby tartan rug was a baby. Little fists and arms had struggled free, and the crumpled face was marked with cold. Chilling moisture clung to its skin, to the knitted bonnet, to the tiny, aimlessly groping hands. So heartbreakingly frail, it had to be newborn.

'Oh, my God!' Gerry said, scooping up the baby, box and all, as it gave another weak wail. 'Don't do that, darling,' she soothed. 'Come on, let's get you inside.'

Carefully she carried it indoors, kicked the door closed behind her, and headed into the kitchen, at this time of day the warmest room in the old kauri villa. She set the box on the table and raced into the laundry to grab a towel and her best cashmere jersey from the hot water cupboard.

'I'll ring the police when I've got you warm,' she promised the baby, lifting it out and carrying it across to the bench. The baby let out another high-pitched wail.

Crooning meaningless words, Gerry stripped the clothes from the squirming body. It was, she discovered, a girl—and judging by the umbilical cord no older than a couple of days, if that.

'I'm going to have to find you some sort of nappy,' she said, cuddling the chilly baby against her breasts as she cocooned it first in cashmere and then the warm towel. 'I wonder how long you've been out there, poppet? Too long on a bitter winter morning. I hope your mother gave you some food before she abandoned you. No, don't cry, sweetheart, don't cry...'

But the baby did cry, face going alarmingly scarlet and her chest swelling as she shrieked her outrage.

Rocking and hushing, Gerry tried to lend the warmth of her body to the fragile infant and wondered whether she should bathe her, or whether that might make her colder. She pressed her cheek against the little head, relieved to find that it seemed marginally warmer.

The front door clicked open and the second member of the household demanded shrilly, 'What's on *earth's* going on?'

Two pairs of feet made their way down the hall, the busy clattering of Cara's high heels counterpointed by a long stride, barely audible on the mellow kauri boards.

It's not my business if she spends the night with a man—she's twenty, Gerry thought, propping the baby against her shoulder and patting the narrow back. The movement silenced the baby for a second, but almost immediately she began to cry again, a pathetic shriek that cut Cara's voice off with the speed of a sword through cheese.

She appeared in the doorway, red hair smoothed back from her face, huge eyes goggling. 'Gerry, what have you done?' she gasped.

'It's a baby,' Gerry said, deadpan, expertly supporting the miniature head with its soft dark fuzz of hair. 'Someone dumped her on the front lawn.'

'Have you rung the police?' Not Cara. The voice was deep and cool, with an equivocal note that made Gerry think of a river running smoothly, forcefully over hidden rocks.

Startled, she looked past Cara to the man who followed her into the room.

Not Cara's usual type, Gerry thought, her stomach suddenly contracting. Her housemate liked pretty television actors and media men, but this man was far from pretty. The stark framework of his face created an aura of steely power, and he looked as though he spent his life dealing with the worst humanity could produce. His voice rang with an authentic authority, warning everyone within earshot that he was in the habit of giving orders and seeing them obeyed.

'I was just about to,' Gerry said stiffly. Irritatingly, the words sounded odd—uneven and hesitant—and she lifted her chin to cover her unusual response.

Gerry had perfected her technique for dealing with men—a lazy, flirtatious approach robbed of any element of sexuality. Instinct warned her that it wasn't going to work with this man; flirting with him, she thought, struggling for balance, would be a hazardous occupation indeed.

A green gaze, clear and cold and glinting like emeralds under water, met hers. Set beneath heavy lids and bordered by thick black lashes, the stranger's eyes were startlingly beautiful in his harsh, compelling face. He took up far too much room in her civilised house, and when he moved towards the telephone it was with a swift, noiseless preci-

sion that reminded Gerry of the predatory grace of a hunt-
ing animal.

Lord, but he was big! Gerry fought back a gut-level appreciation of just how tall he was as he dialled, recounted
the situation with concise precision, gave a sharp inclina-
tion of his tawny head, and hung up. 'They'll call a social
worker and get here as soon as they can. Until then they
suggest you keep it warm.'

'Her,' Gerry corrected, cuddling the baby closer. It snuf-
fled into silence and turned its head up to her, one eye
screwed shut, small three-cornered mouth seeking nourish-
ment. 'No, sweetheart, there's nothing here for you,' she
said softly, her heart aching for the helpless child, and for
the mother desperate enough to abandon her.

'You look quite at home with a baby,' Cara teased, recovering from astonishment into her natural ebullience.

Gerry gave her a fleeting grin. 'You've lived here long
enough to know that I've got cousins from here to glory,
most of whom seem to have had babies in the past three
years. I'm a godmother twice over, and reasonably hands-
on.'

The baby began to wail again, and Cara said uncertainly,
'Couldn't we give it some milk off a spoon, or something?'

'You don't give newborn babies straight cows' milk. But
if someone could go to the dairy—I know they sell babies'
bottles there; I saw a woman buy one when I collected the
bread the other day—we could boil some water and give it
to her.'

'Will that be safe?' the strange man asked, his lashes
drooping slightly.

Gerry realised that her face was completely bare of cosmetics; furthermore, she wore only her dressing gown—her
summer dressing gown, a thin cotton affair that probably
wasn't hiding the fact that she was naked beneath it. 'Safer
than anything else, I think. Here,' she said, offering the
baby to Cara, 'hold her for a moment, will you?'

The younger woman recoiled. 'No, I can't, I've never

held a baby in my life. She's so tiny! I might drop her, or break an arm or something.'

'I'll take her,' the green-eyed stranger said crisply, and did so, scooping the child from Gerry's arms with a sure deftness that reassured her. He looked at Cara. 'Put the kettle on first, then go to the dairy and buy a feeding bottle. My car keys are in my right pocket.'

She pouted, but gave him a flirtatious glance from beneath her lashes as she removed the keys. 'You trust me with your car? I'm honoured. Gerry, it's a stunning black Jag, one of the new ones.'

'And if you hit anything in it,' the man said, with a smile that managed to be both sexy and intimidating, 'I'll take it out of your hide.'

Cara giggled, swung the keys in a little circle and promised, 'I'll be careful. I'm quite a good driver, aren't I, Gerry?' She switched her glance to Gerry and stopped, eyes and mouth wide open. 'Gerry!'

'What?' she asked, halfway to the door.

Cara said incredulously, 'You haven't got any make-up on! I've never seen you without it before!'

'It happens,' Gerry said, and managed to slow her rush to a more dignified pace. At the door, however, she turned and said reluctantly, 'She hasn't got a napkin on.'

'It wouldn't be the first time a baby's wet me,' he said drily. 'I think I can cope.'

Oh, boy, Gerry thought, fleeing after an abrupt nod. I'll just bet you can cope with *anything* fate throws at you. Ruler of your destiny, that's you, whoever you are! No doubt he had another expensive dark suit at his office, just in case he had an accident!

In her bedroom she tried to concentrate on choosing clothes, but she kept recalling the impact of that hard-hewn face and those watchful, speculative eyes.

And that smile. As the owner of a notorious smile herself, Gerry knew that it gave her an undeserved edge in the battle of the sexes. This man's smile transformed his harsh features, honing the blatant male magnetism that came with broad shoulders and long legs and narrow hips and a height of close to six foot four.

It melted her backbone, and he hadn't even been smiling at her!

Where on earth had Cara found him?

Or, given his aura of masterful self-possession, where had *he* found *her*?

The younger woman's morals were no concern of hers, but for some reason Gerry wished that Cara hadn't spent the night with him.

Five minutes later she'd pulled on black trousers and ankle boots, and a neat pinstriped shirt in her favourite black and white, folded the cuffs back to above her wrist, and looped a gold chain around her throat. A small gold hoop hung from each ear. Rapidly she applied a thin coat of tinted moisturiser and lip-glaze.

Noises from outside had indicated Cara's careful departure, and slightly more reckless return. With a touch of defiance, Gerry delicately smoothed a faint smudge of eye-shadow above each dark blue-green eye. There, she told her reflection silently, the mask's back in place.

Once more her usual sensible, confident self, she walked down the hall to the living room. Previous owners had renovated the old villa, adding to the lean-to at the back so that what had been a jumble of small rooms was now a large kitchen, dining and living area.

The bookcases that lined one wall had been Gerry's contribution to the room, as were the books in them and the richly coloured curtains covering French windows. Outside, a deck overlooked a garden badly in need of renovation— Gerry's next project. It should have been finished by now, but she'd procrastinated, drawing endless plans, because once she got it done she might find herself restlessly looking around for something new to occupy herself.

Cara was sitting beside the man on one of the sofas, gazing into his face with a besotted expression.

Had Gerry been that open and easy to read at twenty? Probably, she thought cynically.

As she walked in the stranger smiled down at the baby lost in his arms. Another transformation, Gerry thought, trying very hard to keep her balance. Only this one was pure tenderness. Whoever he was, the tawny-haired man was able to temper his great strength to the needs of the weak.

The man looked up. Even cuddling a baby, he radiated a compelling masculinity that provoked a flicker of visceral caution. It was the eyes—indolent yet perceptive—and the dangerous, uncompromising face.

After some worrying experiences with men in her youth, Gerry had carefully and deliberately developed a persona that was a mixture of open good humour, light flirtation, and warm charm. Men liked her, and although many found her attractive they soon accepted her tacit refusal to be anything other than a friend. Few cared to probe beneath the pleasant, laughing surface, or realised that her slow, lazy smile hid heavily guarded defences.

Now, with those defences under sudden, unsparing assault—all the more dangerous because she was fighting a hidden traitor in her own body and mind—she was forced to accept that she'd only been able to keep men at a distance because she'd never felt so much as a flicker of attraction.

'Flicker' didn't even begin to describe the white-hot flare of recognition that had seared through her when she first laid eyes on the stranger, a clamorous response that both appalled and embarrassed her.

Hiding her importunate reaction with a slightly strained version of her trademark smile, she asked, 'How's she been?'

'She's asleep,' he said, watching her with an unfaltering, level gaze that hid speculation and cool assessment in the green depths.

Something tightened in Gerry's stomach. Most men

preened under her smile, wrongly taking a purely natural movement of tiny muscles in her face as a tribute to their masculinity. Perhaps because he understood the power of his own smile, this man was immune to hers.

Or perhaps he was immune to her. She wouldn't like him for an enemy, she thought with an involuntary little shiver.

The baby should have looked incongruous in his arms, but she didn't. Blissfully unconscious, her eyes were dark lines in her rosy little face. From time to time she made sucking motions against the fist at her mouth.

'We haven't been introduced,' Gerry said. Relieved that his hands were occupied with the baby, she kept hers by her sides. 'I'm Gerry Dacre.'

'Oh, sorry,' Cara said, opening her eyes very wide. 'Gerry's my agent, Bryn, and she owns the house—her aunt's my mother's best friend, and for her sins she said she'd board me for a year.' She gave a swift urchin grin. 'Gerry, this is Bryn Falconer.'

Exquisitely beautiful, Cara was an up-and-coming star for the modelling agency Gerry part-owned. And she was far too young for Bryn Falconer, whose hard assurance indicated that his thirty-two or three years had been spent in tough places.

'How do you do, Bryn?' Gerry said, relying on formality. 'I'll sterilise the bottle—'

'Cara organised that as soon as she came in,' he said calmly.

'Mr Patel said that the solution he gave me was the best way to disinfect babies' bottles,' Cara told her. 'I followed the instructions exactly.'

Sure enough, the bottle was sitting in a special basin on the bench. Gerry gave a swift, glittering smile. 'Good. How long does it have to stay in the solution?'

'An hour,' Cara said knowledgeably. She glanced at the tiny bundle sleeping in Bryn's arms. 'Do you think she'll be all right until then?'

Gerry nodded. 'She should be. She's certainly not hungry now, or she wouldn't have stopped crying. I'll make a much-needed cup of coffee.' Her stomach lurched as she met the measuring scrutiny of Bryn Falconer's green eyes. 'Can I get you one, or some breakfast?' Cara didn't drink coffee, and vowed that breakfast made her feel ill.

The corners of his long, imperious mouth lifted slightly. 'No, thank you.' He transferred his glance to Cara's face and smiled. 'Don't you have to get ready for work?'

'Yes, but I can't leave you holding the baby!' Giggling, she flirted her lashes at him.

Disgusted, Gerry realised that she felt left out. Stiffly she reached for the coffee and began the pleasant routine of making it.

From behind her Bryn said, 'I don't run the risk of losing my job if I'm late.'

Cara cooed, 'It must be wonderful to be the boss.'

Trying very hard to make her voice steady, Gerry said, 'Cara, you can't be late for your go-see.'

'I know, I know.' Reluctance tinged her voice.

Gerry's mouth tightened. Cara really had it bad; last night she'd been over the moon at her luck. Now, as though a chance to audition for an international firm meant nothing to her, she said, 'I'd better change, I suppose.'

Gerry reached for a cup and saucer. Without looking at him, she said, 'You don't have to stay, Mr Falconer. I'll look after the baby until the police come.'

'I'm in no hurry,' he replied easily. 'Cara, if you're ready in twenty minutes I'll give you a lift into Queen Street.'

'Oh—that'd be wonderful!'

Swinging around, Gerry said grittily, 'This is a really important interview, Cara.'

'I know, I know.' Chastened, Cara sprang to her feet. 'I'll wear exactly what we decided on.'

She walked around Bryn's long legs and set out for the door, stopping just inside it when he asked Gerry, 'Don't you have to work too?'

Cara said, 'Oh, Gerry's on holiday, lucky thing. Although,' she added fairly, 'it's her first holiday since she started up the agency three years ago.'

'You're very young, surely, to be running a model agency?'

Although neither Bryn's words nor his tone gave anything away, Gerry suspected he considered her job lightweight and frivolous. Her eyes narrowed slightly, but she gave him her smile again and said, 'How kind of you. What do you do, Mr Falconer?'

Cara hovered, her lovely face bemused as she looked from one to the other.

'Call me Bryn,' he invited, hooded eyes gleaming behind those heavy lashes.

'Thank you, Bryn,' Gerry said politely, and didn't reciprocate. His smile widened into a swift shark's grin that flicked her on the raw. In her most indolent voice Gerry persisted, 'And what do you do?'

The grin faded as rapidly as it had arrived. 'I'm an importer,' he said.

Cara interrupted, 'I'll see you soon, Bryn.'

Bryn Falconer's gaze didn't follow her out of the room. Instead he looked down at the sleeping baby in his arms, and then up again, catching Gerry's frown as she picked up the package of sterilising preparation.

'Gerry doesn't suit you,' he said thoughtfully. 'Is it your real name?'

Gerry's brows shot up. 'Actually, no,' she drawled, emphasising each syllable a little too much. 'It's Geraldine, which doesn't suit me either.'

His smile had none of the sexy warmth that made it so alarmingly attractive. Instead there was a hint of ruthlessness in it as his gaze travelled with studied deliberation over her face. 'Oh, I don't know about that. ''The fair Geraldine'',' he quoted, astonishing her. 'I think it suits you very well. You're extremely beautiful.' His glance lingered on the flakes of colour across her high cheekbones. Softly he said, 'You have a charming response to compliments.'

'I'm not used to getting them first thing in the morning,' she said, angry at the struggle it took her to achieve her usual poised tone.

His lashes drooped. 'But those compliments are the sweetest,' he said smoothly.

Oh, he knew how to make a woman blush—and he'd made the sexual implication with no more than a rasp in the deep voice that sent a shivering thrill down her spine, heat and cold intermingled. Into her wayward mind flashed an image of him naked, the big limbs slack with satisfied desire, the hard, uncompromising mouth blurred by kisses.

No doubt he'd woken up like that this morning, but it had been Cara's kisses on his mouth, Cara's sleek young body in his arms.

Repressing a sudden, worrying flare of raw jealousy, Gerry parried, 'Well, thank you. I do make excellent breakfasts, but although I'm always pleased to receive compliments on my cooking—' her voice lingered a moment on the word before she resumed, '—I don't know that I consider them the *sweetest*. Most women prefer to be complimented on more important qualities.' Before he had a chance to answer she switched the subject. 'You know, the baby's sleeping so soundly—I'm sure she wouldn't wake if I took her.'

It was the coward's way out and he had to know it, but he said calmly, 'Of course. Here you are.'

Gerry realised immediately that she had made a mistake. Whereas they'd transferred the baby from her arms to his in one swift movement, now it had to be done with slow care to avoid waking her.

Bryn's faint scent—purely male, with a slight, distasteful flavouring of Cara's favourite tuberose—reached right into a hidden, vulnerable place inside Gerry. She discovered that the arms that held the baby were sheer muscle, and that the faint shadow of his beard beneath his skin affected her in ways she refused even to consider.

And she discovered that the accidental brush of his hand against her breasts sent a primitive, charged thrill storming through her with flagrant, shattering force.

'Poor little scrap!' she said in a voice too even to be natural, when the child was once more in her arms. Turning away, she fought for some composure. 'I wonder why her mother abandoned her. The usual reason, I suppose.'

'Is there a usual reason?' His voice was level and condemnatory. 'How would you know? The mothers in these cases aren't discovered very often.'

'I've always assumed it's because they come from homes where being an unmarried mother is considered wicked, and they're terrified of being found out.'

'Or perhaps because the child is a nuisance,' he said.

Gerry gave him a startled look. Hard green eyes met hers, limpid, emotionless. Looking down, she thought, He's far too old for Cara! before her usual common sense reasserted itself.

'This is a newborn baby,' she said crisply. 'Her mother won't be thinking too clearly, and could quite possibly be badly affected mentally by the birth. Even so, she left her where she was certain to be noticed and wrapped her warmly. She didn't intend her to die.'

'Really?' He waited a moment—making sure, she wondered with irritation, that she knew how to hold the baby?—before stepping back.

Cuddling the child, Gerry sat down on the opposite sofa, saying with brazen nerve, 'You seem very accustomed to children. Do you have any of your own?'

'No,' he said, his smile a thin line edged with mockery. 'Like you, I have friends with families, and I can claim a couple of godchildren too.'

Although he hadn't answered her unspoken question, he knew what she'd been asking. If she wanted to find out she was going to have to demand straight out, Are you married?

And she couldn't do that; Cara's love life was her own business. However, Gerry wondered whether it might be a good idea to drop a few comments to her about the messiness of relationships with married men.

Apart from anything else, it made for bad publicity, just the sort Cara couldn't afford at the beginning of her career.

She was glad when the sudden movement of the baby in her arms gave her an excuse to look away. 'All right, little love,' she soothed, rocking the child until she settled back into deep sleep.

He said, 'Your coffee's finished percolating. Can I pour it for you?'

'Thank you,' she said woodenly.

'My pleasure.' He got to his feet.

Lord, she thought wildly, he towers! From her perch on the sofa the powerful shoulders and long, lean legs made him a formidable, intimidating figure. Although a good height for a model, Cara had looked tiny beside him.

'Are you sure you don't want one?'

'Quite sure, thanks. Will you be able to drink it while you're holding the baby?'

What on earth had she been thinking of? 'I hadn't—no, I'd better not,' she said, wondering what was happening to her normally efficient brain.

'I'll pour it, anyway. If it's left too long on a hotplate it stews. I can take the baby back while you drink.' He spoke pleasantly.

Gerry tried not to watch as he moved easily around her kitchen, but it was impossible to ignore him because he had so much presence, dominating the room. Even when she looked out of the window at the grey and grumpy dawn doing its ineffectual best to banish the darkness, she was acutely aware of Bryn Falconer behind her, his presence overshadowing her thoughts.

'There.' He put the coffee mug down on the table before her, lean, strong hands almost a dramatic contrast to its blue and gold and white stripes. 'Do you take sugar or milk?'

'Milk, thank you.'

He straightened, looking down at her with gleaming, enigmatic eyes. 'I'm surprised,' he said, his voice deliberate yet disturbing. 'I thought you'd probably drink it black.'

She gave him the smile her cousins called 'Gerry's offensive weapon'. Slow, almost sleepy, it sizzled through men's defences, one of her more excitable friends had told her, like maple syrup melting into pancakes.

Bryn Falconer withstood it without blinking, although his eyes darkened as the pupils dilated. Savagely she thought, So you're not as unaffected as you pretend to be, and then realised that she was playing with fire—dangerous, frightening, peculiarly fascinating fire.

In a crisp, frosty voice, she said, 'Stereotyping people can get you into trouble.'

He looked amused and cynical. 'I must remember that.'

Gerry repressed a flare of anger and said in a languid social tone, 'I presume you were at the Hendersons' party last night?' And was appalled to hear herself; she sounded like a nosy busybody. He'd be quite within his rights to snub her.

He poured milk into her coffee. Gerry drew in a deep, silent breath. It was a cliché to wonder just how hands would feel on your skin, and yet it always happened when you were attracted to someone. How unfair, the advantage a graceful man had over a clumsy one.

And although graceful seemed an odd word to use for a man as big as Bryn Falconer she couldn't think of a better one. He moved with a precise, assured litheness that pleased the eye and satisfied some inner need for harmony.

'I met Cara there,' he said indifferently.

Feeling foolish, because it was none of her business and she knew it, Gerry ploughed on, 'Cara's very young.'

'You sound almost maternal,' he said, his expression inflexible, 'but you can't be more than a few years older than she is.'

'Nine, actually,' Gerry returned. 'And Cara has lived in

the country all her life; any sophistication comes from her years at boarding school. Not exactly a good preparation for real life.'

'She seems mature enough.'

For what? Gerry wondered waspishly. A flaming affair? Hardly; it would take a woman of considerable worldly experience to have an affair with Bryn Falconer and emerge unscathed.

He looked down at the baby, still sleeping peacefully, and asked, 'Do you want me to take her while you drink your coffee?'

The coffee could go cold and curdle for all she cared; Gerry had no intention of getting close to him again. It was ridiculous to be so strongly aware of a man who not only indulged in one-night stands, but liked women twelve or so years younger than he was. 'She'll be all right on the sofa,' she said, and laid her down, keeping a light hand on the child as she picked up the mug and held it carefully well away from her.

Sitting down opposite them, he leaned back and surveyed Gerry, his wide, hard mouth curled in a taunting little smile.

I don't like you at all, Bryn Falconer, Gerry thought, sipping her coffee with feigned composure. The bite of the caffeine gave her the impetus to ask sweetly, 'What sort of things do you import, Mr Falconer?'

'Anything I can earn a penny on, Ms Dacre,' he said, mockery shading his dark, equivocal voice. 'Clothing, machinery, computers.'

'How interesting.'

One brow went up. 'I suppose you have great difficulty understanding computers.'

'What's to understand?' she said in her most come-hither tone. 'I know how to use them, and that's all that matters.'

'You did warn me about the disadvantages of stereotyping,' he murmured, green gaze raking her face. 'Perhaps I should take more notice of what you say. The face of an

angel and a mind like a steel trap. How odd to find you the
owner of a model agency.'

'Part-owner. I have a partner,' she purred. 'I like pretty
things, and I enjoy pretty people.' She didn't intend to tell
him that she was already bored with running the agency.
She'd enjoyed it enormously while she and Honor
McKenzie were setting it up and working desperately to
make it a success, but now that they'd made a good name
for themselves, and an excellent income, the business had
lost its appeal.

As, she admitted rigorously, had everything else she'd
ever done.

A thunderous knock on the door woke the baby. Jerking
almost off the sofa, she opened her triangular mouth and
shrieked. 'That's probably the police,' Gerry said, setting
her cup down and scooping the child up comfortingly. 'Let
them in, will you?' Her voice softened as she rocked the
tiny form against her breast. 'There, darling, don't cry,
don't cry…'

Bryn got to his feet and walked out, his mouth disci-
plined into a straight line. Gazing down at the wrathful face
of the baby, Gerry thought wistfully that although she
didn't want to get married, it would be rather nice to have
a child. She had no illusions—those cousins who'd embarked on marriage and motherhood had warned her that
children invariably complicated lives—but she rather suspected that her biological clock was ticking. 'Shh, shh,' she
murmured. 'Just wait a moment and I'll give you some
water to drink.'

The baby settled down, reinforcing Gerry's suspicion
that she'd been fed not too long before she'd been found.

Frowning, she listened as Bryn Falconer said firmly from
the hall, 'No, I don't live here; I'm just passing through.'

Policemen were supposed to have seen it all, but the one
who walked in through the kitchen door looked startled
and, when his gaze fell on Gerry, thunderstruck.

'This,' Bryn said smoothly, green eyes snapping with

mockery, 'is Constable Richards. Constable, this is Geraldine Dacre, the owner of the house, who found the child outside on the lawn.'

'How do you do?' Gerry said, smiling. 'Would you like a cup of coffee?'

'I—ah, no, thank you, Ms Dacre.' His collar seemed to be too tight; tugging at it, he said, 'I was supposed to meet a social worker here.'

'She—or he—hasn't arrived yet.' Bryn Falconer was leaning against the doorpost.

For all the world as though this was his house! Smiling at the policeman again, Gerry said, 'If you have to wait, you might as well have something to drink—it's cold out there. Bryn, pour the constable some coffee, would you?'

'Of course,' he said, the green flick of his glance branding her skin as he strode behind the breakfast bar.

He hadn't liked being ordered around. Perhaps, she thought a trifle smugly, in the future he wouldn't be quite so ready to take over.

What the hell was she thinking? She had no intention of letting Bryn Falconer into her life.

CHAPTER TWO

HASTILY Gerry transferred her attention to the policeman. 'What do you want to know about the baby?' she asked. 'She's a little girl, and although I'm no expert I don't think she's any more than a day old, judging by the umbilical cord.'

He gave her a respectful look and rapidly became professional. 'Exactly what time did you first see her?' he said.

So, very aware of the opening and closing of cupboards in her kitchen, Gerry explained how she'd found the child, nodding at the box with its pathetic little pile of damp clothes. The policeman asked pertinent questions and took down her answers, thanking Bryn Falconer when he brought a mug of coffee.

The constable plodded through his cup of coffee and his questions until Cara appeared in the doorway, her sultry face alive with curiosity and interest.

'Hello,' she said, and watched with the eye of a connoisseur as the policeman leapt to his feet. 'I'm ready to go,' she told Bryn, her voice soft and caressing. 'Bye, Gerry. Have fun.'

Bryn smiled, the crease in his cheek sending an odd frisson straight through Gerry. Go now, she commanded mentally. Right now. And flushed as he looked at her, a hard glint in his eyes.

Fortunately the doorbell pealed again, this time heralding the social worker, a pleasant, middle-aged woman with tired eyes and a knack with babies. Cara and Bryn left as she came in, so Gerry could give all her attention to the newcomer.

'I'm rather sad to see her go,' Gerry said, watching as

the woman efficiently dressed the baby in well-worn but pretty clothes, then packed her into an official carrycot while the policeman took the box and its contents. 'For what it's worth, I think her mother fed her before she put her behind the hedge—she's not hungry. And she wasn't very cold when I picked her up, so she hadn't been there long.'

The social worker nodded. 'They usually make sure someone will find them soon.'

Gerry picked up her towel and the still dry cashmere jersey. 'What will happen to the baby?'

'Now? I'll get her checked over medically, and take her to a family who'll foster her until her mother is found.'

'And if her mother isn't found?'

The social worker smiled. 'We'll do our best for her.'

'I know,' Gerry said. 'I just feel a bit proprietary.'

'Oh, we all do that.' The woman gave a tired, cynical smile. 'When you think we're geared by evolution to respond to a baby's cry with extreme discomfort, it's no wonder. She'll be all right. It's the mother I'm worried about. I don't suppose you've seen a pregnant woman looking over the hedge this last couple of weeks, or anything like that?'

'No, not a glimpse.'

The policeman said, 'I'd say she's local, because she put the baby where she was certain she'd be found. She might even have been watching.'

Gerry frowned, trying to recall the scene. 'I don't think so. Apart from the traffic, I didn't see any movement.'

When they'd gone she lifted the cashmere jersey to her face. It smelt, she thought wryly, of newborn baby—that faint, elusive, swiftly fading scent that had probably once had high survival value for the human race. Now it was just another thing, along with the little girl's heart-shaking fragility and crumpled rose-petal face, to remind Gerry of her empty heart.

'Oh, do something sensible instead of moping,' she advised herself crisply, heading for the laundry.

After she'd dealt with the clothes she embarked on a brisk round of necessary housework that didn't ease her odd flatness. Clouds settled heavily just above the roof, and the house felt chilly. And empty.

Ruthlessly she banished the memory of wide shoulders, narrow masculine hips and a pair of gleaming green eyes, and set to doing the worst thing she could find—clearing out the fridge. When she'd finished she drank a cup of herbal tea before picking up the telephone.

'Jan?' she said when she'd got through. 'How are you?'

'I'm fine,' said her favourite cousin, mother of Gerry's goddaughter, 'and so are Kear and Gemma, but why aren't you at work?'

'How do you know I'm not?'

'No chaos in the background,' Jan said succinctly. 'The agency is mayhem.'

'Honor persuaded me to take a holiday—she said three years without one was too long. And she was right. I've been a bit blasé lately.'

'I wondered how long you'd last,' Jan said comfortably. 'I told Kear a month or so ago that it must be time for you to look around for something new.'

'Butterfly brain, that's me.'

'Don't be an idiot.' For a tiny woman Jan could be very robust. 'You bend your not inconsiderable mental energy to mastering something, and as soon as you've done it you find something else. Nothing butterfly about that. Anyway, if I remember correctly it was your soft heart that got you into the modelling business. You left the magazine because you didn't agree with the way it was going—and you were right; it's just appalling now, and I refuse to buy it—and Honor needed an anchor after she broke up with that awful man she was living with. Whatever happened to him?'

'He died of an overdose. He was a drug addict.'

'What a tragedy,' Jan sighed. 'If you're on the lookout for another job, will you stay in the fashion industry?'

'It's a very narrow field,' Gerry said, wondering why she now yearned for wider horizons. She'd been perfectly happy working in or on the fringes of that world since she'd left university.

'Well, if you're stuck you can take over from me.'

'In which capacity—babysitter, part-time image consultant, or den mother to a pack of wayward girls?'

Several years previously Jan had inherited land from her grandfather in one of Northland's most beautiful coastal areas, and had set up a camp for girls at risk. After marrying the extremely sexy man next door, she'd settled into her new life as though she'd been born for it.

Jan laughed. 'The camp is going well,' she said cheerfully, 'but I don't think it's you. I meant as image consultant. You'd be good at it—you know what style means because you've got it right to your bones, and you like people. I've had Maria Hastings working for me, but she, wretched woman, has fallen in love with a Frenchman and is going to live in Provence with him! And I'm pregnant again, which forces the issue. I sell, or I retire. I'd rather sell the business to you if you've got the money.'

'Well—congratulations!' It hurt. Stupid, but it hurt. Jan had everything—an adoring husband, an interesting career, a gorgeous child and now the prospect of another. Quickly, vivaciously, Gerry added, 'I'll think about it. If I decide to do it, my share of the agency should be enough to buy you out.'

'Have you spoken to Honor? Does she mind the thought of you leaving?'

'No. Apparently she's got a backer, and she'll buy my share at a negotiated price.'

'I don't want to over-persuade you,' Jan said quickly. 'I know you like to develop things for yourself, so don't feel obliged to think about it. Another woman wants it, and she'll do just as well. You're a bit inclined to let the people you like push you around, you know. Too soft-hearted.'

'You're not over-persuading.' Already the initial glow of enthusiasm was evaporating. What would happen when she got tired of being an image consultant? As she would. A shiver of panic threaded through her. Surely that wasn't to be her life? Her mother had spent her short life searching for something, and had failed spectacularly to find it. Gerry was determined not to do the same.

'Something wrong?' Jan asked.

'Nothing at all, apart from an upsetting start to my day.' She told her about the abandoned baby, and they discussed it for a while, until Gerry asked, 'When's your baby due?'

'In about seven months. What's the matter, Gerry?'

'Nothing. Just—oh, I suppose I do need this holiday. I'll let you know about the business,' Gerry said.

'Do you want to come up and stay with us? We'd love to see you.'

'It sounds lovely, but no, I think I want to wander a bit.'

Jan's tone altered. 'Feeling restless?'

'Yes,' she admitted.

'Don't worry,' Jan said in a bracing voice. 'Even if you don't buy my business a job will come hopping along saying, Take me, take me. I'm fascinating and fun and you'll love me. Why don't you go overseas for a couple of weeks—somewhere nice and warm? I don't blame you for being out of sorts; I can't remember when New Zealand's had such a wet winter.'

'My mother used to go overseas whenever life got into too tedious a routine,' Gerry said.

'You are *not* like your mother,' Jan said even more bracingly. 'She was a spoilt, pampered brat who never grew up. You are a darling.'

'Thank you for those kind words, but I must have ended up with some of her genes.'

'You got the face,' Jan said drily. 'And the smile—but you didn't get the belief that everyone owed you a life.

According to my mama, Aunt Fliss was spoilt stupid by her father, and she just expected the rest of the world to treat her the way he did. You aren't like that.'

'I hope not.'

'Not a bit. Gerry, I have to go—your goddaughter is yelling from her bedroom, and by the tone of her voice it's urgent. I'll ring you tonight and we can really gossip. As for a new job—well, why not think PR? You know everyone there is to know in New Zealand, and you'd be wonderful at it. One flash of that notorious smile and people would be falling over themselves to publicise whatever you want.'

'Oh, exaggerate away!' Gerry laughed, but after she'd hung up she stood looking down at the table, tracing the line of the grain with one long finger.

For the last year she'd been fighting a weariness of spirit; it had crept on her so gradually that for months she hadn't realised what it was. *The curse of my life*, she thought melodramatically, and rolled her eyes.

But it terrified her; boredom had driven her mother through three unsatisfactory marriages, leaving behind shattered lives and discarded children as she'd searched for the elusive happiness she'd craved. Gerry's father had never got over his wife's defection, and Gerry had two half-brothers she hardly ever saw, one in France, one in America—both abandoned, just as she'd been.

She sat down with the newspaper, but a sudden scatter of rain against the window sent her fleeing to bring in the clothes she'd hung on the line an hour before.

A quick glance at the sky told her they weren't going to get dry outside, so she sorted them into the drier and set it going. Staring at the tumble of clothes behind the glass door, she wondered if perhaps she *should* go overseas.

Somewhere warm and dry, she thought dourly, heading back to pick up the newspaper from the sofa. The model disporting herself beneath palm trees was one she had worked with several occasions in her time as fashion editor; Gerry was meanly pleased to see that her striking face was at last showing signs of the temper tantrums she habitually engaged in.

'Serves her right, the trollop,' she muttered, flicking the pages over before putting the newspaper down.

No, she wouldn't head overseas. She couldn't really afford it; she had a mortgage to pay. Perhaps she should try something totally different.

She read the Sits Vac with mounting gloom. Nothing there. Well, she could make a right-angle turn and do another degree. She rooted in a drawer for the catalogue of extension courses at the local university, and began reading it.

But after a short while she put it to one side. She felt tired and grey and over the hill, and she wondered what had happened to the baby. Had she been checked, and was she now in the arms of a foster-mother?

Gerry decided to clean the oven.

It was par for the course when halfway through this most despised of chores the telephone beeped imperatively.

An old friend demanded that Gerry come to lunch with her because she was going through a crisis and needed a clear head to give her advice. Heaving a silent sigh, Gerry said soothingly, 'Yes, of course I'll have lunch with you. Would you like to eat here?'

Her hopes were dashed. 'We'll go to The Blue Room,' Troy said militantly. 'I've booked. I'll pick you up in half an hour.'

'No, I'll meet you there,' Gerry said hastily. Troy was the worst driver she knew.

Coincidences, Gerry reflected gloomily, were scary; you had no defence against them because they sneaked up from behind and hit you over the head. Bryn Falconer was sitting at the next table.

'And then,' Troy said, her voice throbbing as it rose from an intense whisper to something ominously close to a screech, 'he said I've let myself go and turned into a cabbage! *He* was the one who *insisted* on having kids and *insisted* I stop work and stay at home with them.'

Fortunately the waiter had taken in the situation and was already heading towards them with a carafe of iced water, a coffee pot and a heaped basket of focaccia bread.

Very fervently Gerry wished that Bryn Falconer had not decided to lunch at this particular restaurant. She was sure she could feel his eyes on her. 'Troy, you idiot, you've been drinking,' she said softly. 'And don't tell me you didn't drink much—it only takes a mouthful in your case.'

'I had to, Gerry. Mrs Landless—my babysitter—had her thirtieth wedding anniversary party last night. Damon wouldn't go so she saved me a glass of champagne.'

'You could have told her that alcohol goes straight to your head. Never mind—have some coffee and bread and you'll soon be fine, and at least you had the sense to come by taxi.'

Her friend's lovely face crumpled. 'Oh, Lord,' she said bitterly, 'I'm making a total *idiot* of myself, and there's bound to be sh-someone who'll go racing off to tell Damon.'

Five years previously Gerry had mentally prophesied disaster when her friend, a model with at least six more years of highly profitable work ahead of her, had thrown it all away to marry her merchant banker. Now she said briskly, 'So, who cares? It's not the end of the world.'

'I *wish* I was like you,' Troy said earnestly and still too loudly. 'You have men falling in love with you all the time, and you just smile that *fabulous* smile and drift on by, breaking hearts without a second thought.'

Acutely aware that Bryn Falconer was sitting close enough to hear those shrill, heartfelt and entirely untrue words, Gerry protested, 'You make me sound like some sort of *femme fatale,* and I'm not.'

'Yes, you are,' Troy argued, fanning her flushed face with her napkin. 'Everyone expects *femmes fatale* to be evil, selfish women, but why should they be? You're so *nice* and you never poach, but *nobody* touches your heart, do they? You don't even *notice* when men fall at your feet. Damon calls you "the unassailable Gerry".'

Gerry glanced up. Bryn Falconer wasn't even pretending not to listen, and when he caught her eyes he lifted his brows in a cool, mockingly level regard that sent frustration boiling through her.

Hastily Gerry looked back at Troy's tragic face. Tamping down an unwise and critical assessment of Damon's character, she said firmly, 'He doesn't know me very well. Have some coffee.'

But although Troy obediently sipped, she couldn't leave the subject alone. 'Have you ever been in love, Gerry? I mean really in love, the sort of abject, dogged, I-love-you-just-because-you're-you sort of love?'

Gerry hoped that her shrug hid her burning skin. 'I don't believe in that sort of love,' she said calmly. 'I think you have to admire and respect someone before you can fall in love with them. Anything else is lust.'

It was the wrong thing to say, and she knew it as soon as the words left her mouth. Bryn Falconer's presence must have scrambled her brain, she decided disgustedly.

Troy dissolved into tears and groped in her bag for her handkerchief. 'I know,' she wept into it. 'Damon wanted me and now it's gone. He's breaking my heart.'

Gerry leaned over the table and took her friend's hand. 'Do you want to go?' she asked quietly.

'Yes.'

Avid, fascinated stares raked Gerry's back as they walked across to the desk. She'd have liked to ignore Bryn Falconer, but when they approached his table he looked up at her with sardonic green eyes. At least he didn't get to his feet, which would have made them even more conspicuous.

Handsome meant nothing, she thought irrelevantly, when a man had such presence!

'Geraldine,' he said, and for some reason her heart stopped, because that single word on his lips was like a claiming, a primitive incantation of ownership.

Keeping her eyes cool and guarded, she sent him a brief smile. 'Hello, Bryn,' she said, and walked on past.

Fortunately Gerry's custom was valuable, so she and the desk clerk came to an amicable arrangement about the bill for the uneaten food. After settling it, she said, 'I'll drive you home.'

'I don't want to go home.' Troy spoke in a flat, exhausted voice that meant reality was kicking in.

'How long's Mrs Landless able to stay with the children?'

'Until four.' Troy clutched Gerry's arm. 'Can I come with you? Gerry, I really need to talk.'

So sorry for Troy she could have happily dumped a chained and gagged Damon into the ocean and watched him gurgle out of sight, Gerry resigned herself to an exhausting afternoon. 'Of course you can.'

Once home, she filled them both up on toast and pea and ham soup from the fridge—comfort food, because she had the feeling they were going to need it.

And three exhausting hours later she morosely ate a persimmon as Troy—by then fully in command of herself—drove off in a taxi.

Not that exhausting was the right word; gruelling described the afternoon more accurately. Although Troy was bitterly unhappy she still clung to her marriage, trying to convince herself that because she loved her husband so desperately, he had to love her in return.

The old, old illusion, Gerry thought sadly and sardonically, and got to her feet, drawing some consolation from her surroundings. She adored her house, revelled in the garden, and enjoyed Cara's company as well as her contribution to the mortgage payments.

But restlessness stretched its claws inside her. Gloomily she surveyed the tropical rhododendrons through her window, their waxy coral flowers defying the grey sky and cold wind. A disastrous lunch, a shattered friend, and the prospect of heavier rain later in the evening didn't mean her holiday was doomed. She wasn't superstitious.

But she wished that Bryn Falconer had chosen to eat lunch anywhere else in New Zealand.

Uncomfortable, jumpy—the way she felt when the music in a horror film indicated that something particularly revolting was about to happen—Gerry set up the ironing board. Jittery nerves wouldn't stand up to the boring, prosaic monotony of ironing.

She was putting her clothes away in her room when she heard the front door open and Cara's voice, bright and lively with an undercurrent of excitement, ring around the hall. The masculine rumble that answered it belonged to Bryn Falconer.

All I need, Gerry thought with prickly resignation.

She decided to stay in her room, but a knock on her door demanded her attention.

'Gerry,' Cara said, flushed, her eyes gleaming, 'come and talk to Bryn. He wants to ask you something.'

Goaded, Gerry answered, 'I'll be out in a minute.'

Fate, she decided, snatching a look at the mirror and despising the colour heating her sweeping cheekbones, really had it in for her today.

However, her undetectable mask of cosmetics was firmly in place, and anyway, she wasn't going to primp for Bryn Falconer. No matter that her dark blue-green eyes were wild and slightly dilated, or that her hair had rioted frivolously out of its usual tamed waves. She didn't care what he thought.

The gas heater in the sitting room warmed the chilly air, but the real radiance came from Cara, who lit up the room like a torch. Should I tell her mother? Gerry thought, then dismissed the idea. Cara was old enough to understand what she was doing.

But that little homily on messing around with married men might be in order.

Not that Bryn looked married—he had the air of someone who didn't have to consider anyone else. Forcing a smile, Gerry said, 'Hello, Bryn. Did you have a good lunch?'

His eyes narrowed slightly. 'Very.'

Gerry maintained her hostess demeanour. 'I like the way they do lunch there—sustaining, and it doesn't make you sleepy in the afternoon.'

'A pity you weren't able to stay long enough to eat,' he said blandly.

Despising the heat in her skin, Gerry kept her voice steady. 'My friend wasn't well.' Before he could comment she continued, 'Cara tells me you want to ask me something?'

'I'd like to offer you a very short, one-off project,' he said, and without giving her time to refuse went on, 'It involves a trip to the islands, and some research into the saleability—or not—of hats.'

Whatever she'd expected it wasn't that. 'Hats,' she repeated blankly.

The green gaze rested a moment on her mouth before moving up to capture her eyes. 'One of the outlying islands near Fala'isi is famous for the hats the islanders weave from a native shrub. They used to bring in an excellent income, but sales are falling off. They don't know why, but I suspect it's because they aren't keeping up with fashion. Cara tells me you have a couple of weeks off. One week at Longopai in the small hotel there should be ample time to check whether I'm right.'

No, she wanted to say, so loudly and clearly that there could be no mistaking her meaning. No, I don't want to go to a tropical island and find out why they're no longer selling their hats. I don't want anything to do with you.

'I'd love to go,' Cara said eagerly, 'but I'm booked solid for a couple of months. You're a real expert, Gerry—you style a shoot better than anyone, and Honor says you've got an instinct about fashion that never lets you down. And you'd have a super time in the islands—it's just what you need.'

Gerry looked out of the window. Darkness had already fallen; the steady drumming of rain formed a background to the rising wail of wind. She said, 'I might not have any idea why they aren't selling. Marketing is—'

'Exactly what you're good at,' Bryn said smoothly, his deep voice sliding with the silky friction of velvet along her nerves. 'When you worked as fashion editor for that magazine you marketed a look, a style, a colour.' He looked around the room. 'You have great taste,' he said.

As Gerry wondered whether she should tell him the room was furnished with pieces from her great-grandmother's estate, he finished, 'I can get you there tomorrow.'

Gerry's brows shot up. It was tempting—oh, she longed to get away and forget everything for a few days, just sink herself into the hedonism of a tropical holiday. Lukewarm lagoons, she thought yearningly, and colour—vivid, primal, shocking colour—and the scent of salt, and the caress of the trade winds on her bare skin...

Aloud, very firmly, she said, 'If you got some photographs done I could probably give you an opinion without going all the way up there. Or you could get some samples.'

'They deal better with people,' he said evenly. 'They'll take one look at you and realise that you know what you're talking about. A written report—or even a suggestion from me—won't have the same impact.'

'Most people,' Cara burbled, 'are dying to get to the tropics at this time of the year. You sound like a wrinklie, Gerry, hating the thought of being prised out of your nice comfortable nest!'

And if I go, Gerry thought with a tiny flash of malice, you'll be alone here, and no one will realise that you're spending nights in Bryn's bed. Although that was unkind;

Cara knew that Gerry wouldn't carry tales to her parents. And she honestly thought she was doing Gerry a favour.

Hell, she probably was.

Green eyes half-closed, Bryn said, 'I'd rather you actually saw the hats. Photographs don't tell the whole story, as you're well aware. And of course the company will pay for your flights and accommodation.'

She was being stupid and she knew it; had any other man suggested it she'd have jumped at the idea. Striving for her usual equanimity, she said, 'Of course I'd like to go, but—'

Cara laughed. 'I told you she wouldn't be able to resist it,' she crowed.

'Where is this island?' Gerry asked shortly.

'Longopai's an atoll twenty minutes by air from Fala'isi.' All business, Bryn said, 'A taxi will pick you up at ten tomorrow morning. Collect your tickets from the Air New Zealand counter at the airport. Pack for a week, but keep in mind the weight restrictions.'

What did he think she was? One of those people who can't leave anything in their wardrobe when they go overseas?

Cara headed off an intemperate reply by breaking in, 'Gerry can pack all she needs for three weeks in an overnight bag,' she said on an awed note.

Bryn's brow lifted. 'Clever Gerry,' he said evenly, his voice expressionless.

So why did it sound like a taunt?

CHAPTER THREE

IT DIDN'T surprise her that Bryn Falconer's arrangements worked smoothly; he'd expect efficiency in his hirelings.

Everything—from the moment Gerry collected her first-class ticket at Auckland airport to the cab-ride through the hot, colourful streets of Fala'isi with the tall young man who'd met the plane—went without a hitch.

'Mr Falconer said you were very important, and that I wasn't to be late,' her escort said when she thanked him for meeting her.

A considerable exaggeration, she thought with a touch of cynicism. Bryn liked her as little as she liked him. 'Do you work for the hotel on Longopai?'

He shook his head. 'For the shipping company. Mr Falconer bought a trader to bring the dried coconut here from Longopai, so it is necessary to have an office here.'

Bryn had said he was an importer—clearly he dealt in Pacific trade goods.

At the waterfront Gerry's escort loaded her and her suitcase tenderly into a float plane. Within five minutes, in a maelstrom of spray and a shriek of engines, the plane taxied out, broke free of the water and rose over the lagoon to cross the white line of the reef and drone north above a tropical sea of such vivid blue-green that Gerry blinked and put on her sunglasses.

She'd forgotten how much she loved the heat and the brilliance, forgotten the blatant, overpowering assault on senses more accustomed to New Zealand's subtler colours and scents. Now, smiling at the large ginger dog of bewildering parentage strapped into the co-pilot's seat, she relaxed.

Between the high island of Fala'isi and the atoll of Longopai stretched a wide strait where shifting colours and surface textures denoted reefs and sandbanks. Gazing down at several green islets, each ringed by blinding coral sand, Gerry wondered how long it would take to go by sea through these treacherous waters.

'Landfall in distant seas,' the pilot intoned dramatically over the intercom fifteen minutes later.

A thin, irregular, plumy green circle surrounded by blinding sand, the atoll enclosed a huge lagoon of enchanting, opalescent blues and greens. To make it perfect, in the centre of the lagoon rested a boat, white and graceful. Not a yacht—too much to expect!—but a large cruiser, some rich man's toy.

Gerry sighed. Oh, she wouldn't want to live on a place like this—too cut off, and, being a New Zealander, she loved the sight of hills on the horizon—but for a holiday what could be better? Sun, sand, and enough of a mission to stop her from becoming inured to self-indulgence.

After a spray-flurried landing in the deeper part of the lagoon, Gerry unbelted as a canoe danced towards them.

'Your transport.' The pilot nodded at it.

Glad that she'd worn trousers and a T-shirt, she pulled on her hat. The canoe surged in against the plane, manned by two young men with dark eyes and the proud features of Polynesians, their grins open and frankly appreciative as they loaded her suitcase.

Amused and touched by the cushion that waited on her seat, Gerry stepped nimbly down, sat gracefully and waved to the pilot. The dog barked and wagged its tail; the pilot said, 'Have a great holiday.'

Yes, indeed, Gerry thought, smiling as the canoe backed away from the plane, swung around and forged across the glittering waters.

New Zealand seemed a long, long way away. For this week she'd forget about it, and the life that had become so terrifyingly flat, to wallow in the delights of doing practically nothing in one of the most perfect climates in the world.

And in one of the most perfect settings!

Following the hotel porter along a path of crushed white shell, Gerry breathed deeply, inhaling air so fresh and languorous it smelt like Eden, a wonderful mixture of the unmatched perfumes of gardenia and frangipani and ylang-ylang, salted by a faint and not unpleasing undernote of fish, she noted cheerfully. Her cabaña, its rustic appearance belying the luxury within, was one of only ten.

'*Very* civilised,' she said aloud when she was alone.

A huge bed draped in mosquito netting dominated one end of the room. Chairs and sofas—made of giant bamboo and covered in the soothing tans and creams of tapa cloth—faced wide windows which had shutters folded back to reveal a deck. Separated from a tiny kitchen by a bar, a wooden table and chairs stood at the other end of the room. Fruit and flowers burst from a huge pottery shell on the table.

Further exploration revealed a bathroom of such unashamed and unregenerate opulence—all marble in soft sunrise hues of cream and pale rose—that Gerry whistled.

Whoever had conceived and designed this hotel had had a very exclusive clientele in mind—the seriously rich who wanted to escape. Although, she thought, eyeing the toiletries laid out on the marble vanity, not too far.

The place was an odd but highly successful blend of sophisticated luxury and romantic, lazy, South Seas simplicity. Normally she'd never be able to afford such a place. She was, she thought happily, going to cost Bryn Falconer megabucks.

Half an hour later, showered and changed into fresh clothes, she strolled down the path, stopping to pick a hibiscus flower and tuck it behind her ear, where its rollicking orange petals and fiery scarlet throat would contrast splendidly with her black curls. Only flowers, she decided, could get away with a colour scheme like that! Or silk, perhaps...

According to the schedule her escort in Fala'isi had given her, she'd have the rest of the day to relax before the serious part of this holiday began. Tomorrow she'd be shown the hats. As the swift purple twilight of the tropics gathered on the horizon, she straightened her shoulders and walked across the coarse grass to the lounge area.

And there, getting up from one of the sinfully comfortable chairs and striding across to meet her, was Bryn Falconer, all power and smooth, co-ordinated litheness, green eyes gleaming with a metallic sheen, his autocratic features only hinting at the powerful personality within.

Gerry was eternally grateful that she didn't falter, didn't even hesitate. But the smile she summoned was pure will-power, and probably showed a few too many teeth, for he laughed, a deep, amused sound that hid any mockery from the three people behind him.

'Hello, Geraldine,' he said, and took her arm with a grip that looked easy. 'Somehow I knew just how you'd look.'

As she was wearing a gentle dress the dark blue-green of her eyes, with a long wrap skirt and flat-heeled sandals, she doubted that very much. Flattering it certainly was—the straight skirt and deep, scooped neckline emphasised her slender limbs and narrow waist—but fashionable it was not.

Arching her brows at him, she murmured, 'Oh? How *do* I look?'

His smile hardened. 'Rare and expensive and fascinating—perfect for a tropical sunset. A moonlit woman, as shadowy and mysterious as the pearls they dive for in one small atoll far to the north of here, pearls the colour of the sea and the sky at midnight.'

Something in his tone—a disturbing strand of intensity, of almost-hidden passion—sent her pulse skipping. Automatically, she deflected.

'What a charming compliment. Thank you,' she returned serenely, dragging her eyes away from the uncompromising authority of his face as he introduced his companions.

Gone was the lingering miasma of ennui; the moment she'd seen him every nerve cell had jolted into acute, almost painful alertness.

Narelle and Cosmo were an Australian couple—sleek, well-tanned, wearing expensive resort clothes. Lacey, their adolescent daughter, should have been rounded and sturdy; instead her angular figure indicated a recent illness.

After the flurry of greetings Gerry sank into the chair Bryn held for her, aware that Lacey was eyeing her with the yearning intensity of a hungry lion confronted by a wildebeest. Uncomfortably, Gerry waited for surnames, but none were forthcoming.

'Isn't this a wonderful place for a holiday?' Narelle, a thin, tanned woman with superbly blonded hair and a lot of gold chains, spoke brightly, her skilfully shaded eyes flicking from Gerry to Bryn.

'Ideal,' Gerry answered, smiling, and was about to add that she wasn't exactly on holiday when Bryn distracted her by asking her what she'd have to drink.

'Fruit juice, thanks,' she said. After the fiasco with Troy she wasn't going to risk anything alcoholic in her empty stomach. She smiled at the waiter who'd padded across on bare feet, and added, 'Not too sweet, please.'

'Papaya, madam? With passionfruit and lime?'

'That sounds wonderful,' she said.

She was oddly uneasy when Lacey said loudly, 'I'll have one of those too, please.'

Her mother gave her a sharp look. 'How about a diet soft drink?' she asked.

'No, thanks.'

Narelle opened her mouth but was forestalled by Bryn, who said, 'Did you have a good flight up, Geraldine?'

Why the devil didn't he use her proper name? 'Geraldine' sounded quite different from her normal, everyday self. 'Yes, thank you,' she said, smiling limpidly.

If he thought that one compliment entitled him to a more intimate footing, he was wrong. All right, so her heart was still recovering from that first sight of him, and for a moment she'd wondered what it would be like to hear that deep voice made raw by passion, but she was strong, she'd get over it.

'We've been here several times,' Narelle said, preening a little. 'Last year Logan Hawkhurst was here with the current girlfriend, Tania Somebody-or-other.'

Logan Hawkhurst was an actor, the latest sensation from London, a magnificently structured genius with a head of midnight hair, bedroom eyes, and a temper—so gossip had it—that verged on molten most of the time.

'And was he as overwhelming as they say?' Gerry asked lightly.

Narelle gave an artificial laugh. 'Oh, more so,' she said. 'Just gorgeous—like something swashbuckling out of history. Lacey had a real a crush on him.'

The girl's face flamed.

Gerry said cheerfully, 'She wasn't the only one. I had to restrain a friend of mine when he finally got married—she wept half a wet Sunday and said she was never going to see another film of his because he'd break her heart all over again.'

They dutifully laughed, and some of the colour faded from the girl's skin.

'Don't know what you women see in him,' Cosmo said, giving Bryn a man-to-man look.

His wife said curtly, 'He's very talented, and you saw quite a lot in his girlfriend, whose talent wasn't so obvious.' She laughed a little spitefully. 'He must like fat women.'

Fortunately the waiter returned with the drinks just then, pale gold and frosted, with moisture sliding down the softly rounded glasses.

Gerry had seen more than enough photographs of the woman Logan Hawkhurst had wooed all over the world and finally won; a tall, statuesque woman, with wide shoulders, glorious legs and substantial breasts, she'd looked as though she was more than capable of coping with a man of legendary temper.

Whatever, Gerry didn't want to deal with undercurrents and sly backbiting. Blast Bryn Falconer. This was not the way she'd envisioned spending her first evening on the atoll.

Even more irritating, Narelle set out to establish territory and pecking order. Possibly Bryn noted the glitter in Gerry's smile, for he steered the conversation in a different direction. Instead of determining who outranked whom, they talked of the latest comet, and the plays on Broadway, and whether cars would ever run on hydrogen. Lacey didn't offer much, but what she did say was sharply perceptive.

Gerry admired the way Bryn handled the girl; he respected her intelligence and treated her as an interesting woman with a lot to offer. Lacey bloomed.

Which was more than Gerry did. Infuriatingly, the confidence she took for granted seemed to be draining away faster than the liquid in her glass. Every time Bryn's hooded green gaze traversed her face her rapid pulse developed an uncomfortable skip, and she had to yank her mind ruthlessly off the question of just how that long, hard mouth would feel against hers...

How foolish of Narelle to try her silly tests of who outranked whom! Bryn was the dominant male, and not only because he was six inches taller than Cosmo; what marked him out was the innate authority blazing around him like a forceful aura, intimidating and omnipresent.

Dragging her attention back, she learned that Cosmo owned a chain of shops in Australia. Narelle turned out to be a demon shopper, detailing the best boutiques in London for clothes, and where to buy gold jewellery, and how wonderful Raffles Hotel in Singapore was now it had been refurbished.

Lacey relapsed into silence, turning her glass in her hand, drinking her fruit juice slowly, as Gerry drank hers, occasionally shooting sideways glances at Bryn. Another crush on the way, Gerry thought, feeling sorry for her.

Politeness insisted she listen to Narelle, nodding and putting in an odd comment, but the other woman was content to talk without too much input from anyone else. From the corner of her eye Gerry noted Bryn's lean, well-shaped hands pick up his beer glass. So acutely, physically aware of him was she that she fancied her skin on that side of her body was tighter, more stretched, than on the other.

'You've travelled quite a bit,' Lacey said abruptly, breaking into her mother's conversation.

'It's part of my job,' Gerry said.

'What do you do?'

She hesitated before saying, 'I work in fashion.'

Lacey looked smug. 'I thought you might be a model,' she said, 'but I *knew* you were something to do with fashion. You've got that look.' She leaned forward. 'Do models have to diet all the time to stay that slim?'

'Thin,' Gerry said calmly. 'They have to be incredibly thin because the camera adds ten pounds to everyone. Some starve themselves, but most don't. They're freaks.'

'F-freaks?' Lacey looked distinctly taken aback.

Bryn asked indolently, 'How many women do you see walking down the street who are six feet tall, skinny as rakes, with small bones and beautiful faces?'

Although the caustic note in his voice stung, Gerry nodded agreement.

'Well—not many, I suppose,' Lacey said defensively.

'It's not normal for women to look like that,' Bryn said with cold-blooded dispassion. 'Gerry's right—those who do are freaks.'

'Designers like women with no curves,' Gerry told her, 'because they show off clothes better.'

Narelle laughed a little shrilly. 'Oh, it's more than that,' she protested. 'Men are revolted by fat women.'

'Some men are,' Bryn said, leaning back in his chair as though he conducted conversations like this every day, 'but most men like women who are neither fat nor thin, just fit and pleasantly curvy.'

So she was not, Gerry realised, physically appealing to him. Although not model-thin, she was certainly on the lean side rather than voluptuous. His implied rejection bit uncomfortably deep; she had, she realised with a shock, taken it for granted that he found her as attractive as she found him.

Lacey asked, 'Are you in fashion too, Mr Falconer?'

'I have interests there,' he said, his tone casual.

Did he mean the hats?

With a bark of laughter Cosmo said, 'Amongst others.'

Bryn nodded. Smoothly, before anyone else could speak, he made some remark about a scandal in Melbourne, and Lacey listened to her parents discuss it eagerly.

Illness or anorexia? Gerry wondered, covertly taking in the stick-like arms and legs. Lacey had her father's build; she should have been rounded. Or just a kid in a growing spurt? Sixteen could be a dangerous age.

Had Bryn discerned that? Why else would he have bothered to warn her off dieting? Because that was what he'd done, in the nicest possible way.

Gerry drained her glass and settled back in her chair, watching the night drift across the sea, sweep tenderly through the palms and envelop everything in a soft, scented darkness. The sound of waves caressing the reef acted as a backdrop; while they'd been talking several other people had come in and sat down, and now a porter was going around lighting flares.

If she were alone, Gerry thought, she'd be having a wonderful time, instead of sitting there with every cell alert and tense, waiting for something to happen.

What happened was that a waiter came across and bent over Bryn, saying cheerfully, 'Your table is ready, sir.'

'Then we'd better eat,' he said, and got to his feet, towering over them. 'Geraldine,' he said, holding out his hand.

Irritated, but unable to reject him without making it too

obvious, Gerry put hers in his and let him help her up, smiling at the others. He kept his grip until they were half-way across the room, when she tugged her fingers free and demanded, 'What on earth is going on?'

'I'd have thought you'd know the signs,' he said caustically. 'If she hasn't got anorexia, she's on the brink.'

'I didn't mean Lacey,' she snapped. 'What are you doing here?'

'I discovered I had a few days, so I decided it would be easier for you if I came up and acted as intermediary.'

Impossible to tell from his expression or his voice whether he was lying, but he certainly wasn't telling the whole story.

'Just like that?' she said, not trying to hide her disbelief. 'You didn't have this time yesterday.'

'Things change,' he told her blandly, pulling out a chair.

He was laughing at her and she resented it, but she wasn't going to make a fool of herself by protesting. So when she'd sat down she seized on the comment he'd made. 'What do you mean, you thought I'd have been able to recognise anorexia?'

'You deal with it all the time, surely?' he said.

She replied bluntly, 'Tragically, anorexic young women who don't get help die. They don't have the stamina to be models.'

'I know they die,' he said, his face a mask of granite, cold and inflexible in the warm, flickering light of the torches. 'How many do you think you've sent down that road?'

His grim question hurt more than a blow to the face.

Before she could defend herself he continued, 'Your industry promotes an image of physical perfection that's completely unattainable for most women. From there it's only a short step to eating disorders.'

'No one knows what causes eating disorders,' she said, uncomfortable because she had worried about this. 'You make it sound as though it's a new thing, but women have always died of eating disorders—they used to call it green sickness or a decline before they understood it. Some psychologists believe it's psychological, to do with personality types, while others think it's caused by lack of control and power. If you men would give up your arrogant assumption of authority over us and appreciate us for what we are—not as trophies to impress your friends and associates—then perhaps we could learn to appreciate ourselves in all our varied and manifold shapes and sizes and looks.'

'That's a cop-out,' he said relentlessly.

She lifted her brows. 'I'm always surprised how responsibility for this has been dumped onto women—magazine editors, writers, models.'

'Are you a feminist, Geraldine?'

The surprise in his voice made her seethe. 'Of course I am,' she said dulcetly. 'Any woman who wants a better life for the next generation of girls is a feminist.'

'Don't you like men?'

'Of *course* I do,' she retorted even more sweetly. 'Some of my best friends are men.'

His smile turned savage. 'Are you trying to be provocative, or does it come naturally to you?'

The taunting question hit her in a vulnerable place. Her father's voice, ghostly, earnest, echoed in her ear. 'Don't tease, Gerry, darling. It's not fair—men don't know how to deal with a woman who teases.'

Banishing it, she counter-attacked. 'Do you think you're the only person who's ever accused me of forcing women into a strait-jacket? Sorry, it happens all the time. Interestingly, no one ever accuses me of forcing the male models into one, or the character models. Just the women.'

He didn't like that; his eyes narrowed to slivers of frigid green.

Strangely stimulated, she went on, 'And with interests in clothing, as well as computers and coconut, don't you think you're being just the tiniest bit hypocritical? After all, some of the money that pays for this fantasy of the South

Pacific—' her swift, disparaging glance scorched around the area '—comes from the women you're so concerned about…those so-called brainwashed followers of fashion.'

As a muscle flicked in the arrogant jaw she thought resignedly, Well, at least I've had half a day in the sun!

But it was something stronger than self-preservation that compelled her to lean forward and say, 'Let's make a bargain, Bryn. You work to stop all the actors and politicians and big businessmen from arming themselves with pretty, slaves-to-fashion trophy women, and I can guarantee that the magazines and fashion industry will fall neatly into line behind you.'

'Are women so driven by what men want?' he asked idly, as though he wasn't furious with her.

A hit. She laughed softly. 'Give us a hundred years of freedom and things will probably be different, but yes, men are important to us and always will be—just as men are affected by women. After all, nature set us up to attract each other.'

'So the desire to find a male with money and prestige is entirely natural, whereas a man's search for a mate who will enhance his prestige is wrong?'

Amusement sparkled in her voice. 'A woman's desire for wealth and prestige is linked, surely, to her instinctive knowledge that her children will have a better chance of surviving if their father is rich and has power in the community? Whereas a man just likes to look good in the eyes of other men!'

Since her university days, Gerry realised, she'd forgotten the sheer pleasure of debating, the swift interchange of ideas intended to provoke, to make people think, not necessarily meant to be taken seriously. Then she made the mistake of looking across the table, and wondered uneasily if for him this was personal. Behind the watchful face she sensed leashed emotions held in check by a formidable will.

'Women want a man who looks good in the eyes of other men,' he retorted. 'You've just said they see losers as bad bets for fatherhood. Besides,' he added silkily, 'surely the reason some men seek younger mates is *their* instinctive understanding that to perpetuate as many of their genes as possible—which is what evolution is all about—they need to mate with as many women as possible? And that young women are more fertile?'

'So men are naturally promiscuous and women naturally look for security?' she challenged. 'Do you believe that, Bryn?'

'As much as you do,' he said ironically, looking past Gerry to the waitress.

Gerry chose fish and a salad; she expected Bryn to be a red meat and potatoes man, but he too decided on fish. She must have looked a little startled because he explained, 'The fish here is one of the natural wonders of the world. And they cook it superbly.'

Those green eyes didn't miss a trick.

From now on she'd be more cautious; no more invigorating arguments or discussions. Even if he was one of the few men who made her blood run faster, she'd be strictly businesslike. She certainly wasn't interested in a man who'd slept with Cara. And who'd then, she realised far too late, had the nerve to trash the modelling industry.

Unless he'd been being as provocative as he'd accused her of being? She shot him an uneasy look, and wondered whether that strong-framed face hid a devious mind.

Possibly. So over a magnificent meal she firmly steered the conversation into dinner-party channels, touching on art, books, public events—nothing personal. Bryn followed suit, yet Gerry found herself absorbed by that intriguing voice with its undercurrent of—what?

It made her think of secrets, his voice—of violent emotions held under such brutal control that the prospect of releasing them assumed the prohibited glamour of the forbidden. It made her think all sorts of tantalising, exciting things.

Fortunately, before she got too carried away, a glance at

his harsh face with its uncompromising aura of power banished those nonsensical thoughts.

This man had no time for subtlety. He probably hadn't been deliberately winding her up with his contempt for models; he'd slept with Cara because he wanted her, and he wouldn't see any contradiction between his words and his behaviour.

Her appetite suddenly leaving her, Gerry looked down at her food.

Bryn Falconer fascinated her, but she knew herself too well—had dreaded for too long the genes that held the seeds of her destruction—to allow herself to act on that excitement.

'Did you see the baby in the newspaper?' he asked.

'Yes, poor wee love, while I was in the first-class lounge waiting for the plane.' And had slipped into sentimentality at the photograph of the crinkled little face, absorbed in sleep. Turning her half-empty glass, she kept her eyes fixed on the shimmering play of light in the crystal. 'The social worker said they'll do their best to find her mother and help her make a home for the child, but if that isn't possible the baby will be adopted. In the meantime she'll be with a foster family.'

'Clock ticking, Geraldine?' he asked. His eyes mocked her.

Repressing the swift, raw antagonism detonated by his lazy percipience, she parried lightly, 'Babies are special. I just hope she has a happy life, and that her mother is able to deal with whatever made her abandon her.'

'You have a kind heart.' An enigmatic note in his dark voice robbed the words of any compliment.

'I am noted for my kindness,' she said evenly. Putting the glass down, she pretended to hide a yawn. 'I'm sorry, I'm tired. Do you mind if I go now?'

'Am I so dull?' he asked with a disconcerting directness.

Startled, she looked up, to be pierced by glinting, sardonic green eyes. 'Not at all,' she said abruptly, antipathy prickling through her veins. Any other man would have accepted her face-saving explanation instead of challenging it.

'It's only nine o'clock. Cara tells me you've been known to stay out all night.'

'Staying out doesn't mean staying up,' she returned tartly, so irritated that Cara should gossip about her that she only realised what she'd implied when his mouth tightened. Almost immediately those firm lips relaxed into a smile that sent complex sensations snaking down her spine.

'Of course not,' he said, drawling the words slightly.

Oh, great, now he thought she was promiscuous. Well, she wasn't going to explain that because she disliked driving at night she tended to borrow a bed when the party looked like running late—and she certainly wasn't going to tell him that she spent the night in those beds alone!

This was a man who'd slept with a woman at least ten years younger than he was. He had no right to look at her like that, with lazy speculation narrowing his eyes.

Getting to her feet, she donned her most serene expression. 'Thank you very much for a lovely meal.'

He rose with her. 'I'll walk you to your room.'

'You don't need to,' she said steadily. 'I'm sure I'm perfectly safe here.'

'Absolutely, unless you consider the flying foxes. They tend to swoop low over the paths and some people find them scary.'

'I don't,' she said, but he came with her anyway.

After a silent walk along the sweet-smelling paths, lit by flares and the moon, he stopped at the door of her chalet while she unlocked it, and said, 'Goodnight, Geraldine.'

'Gerry,' she said before she could stop herself. 'Nobody calls me Geraldine.'

In the soft, treacherous moonlight his face was all angles and planes, an abstract study of strength emphasised by his eyes, their colour bleached to silver, hooded and dangerous. 'Who named you Geraldine?'

Startled, she gave him a direct answer. 'My mother.'

'Did she die young?'

'Oh, yes,' she said flippantly. 'But she'd left me long before she died. She was a bolter, my mother—she got bored easily. She died in a car crash, running away from her third husband to the man who was going to be her fourth.'

'How old were you when she left?'

Past pain, Geraldine had learnt, was best left to the past, but by telling him she'd opened the way for his question. 'Four. That was pretty good, actually. She left my half-brothers before they were able to recognise her.'

'Yet you can find sympathy for the woman who abandoned the baby?'

She shrugged. 'It's always easier to forgive when it's not personal. Besides, my mother made a habit of it, and she left chaos behind her. She had a talent for wrecking lives.'

'Did she wreck yours?' His voice was reflective.

Gerry lifted her head. 'No. I couldn't have asked for a happier childhood—my father devoted himself to me. But he never married again.'

'Then she only wrecked one life,' he pointed out objectively. 'If you don't include hers, of course.'

Reining in a most unusual aggression, Gerry retorted, 'She didn't do much for my half-brothers or their fathers.'

'She sounds more disturbed than malicious.' He stopped abruptly, as though he'd said more than he'd wanted to.

Looking up, Gerry caught the sudden clamping of his features. 'You're right,' she said lightly, mockingly. 'There are always two sides to every question, and we will never know what drove my mother headlong to destruction.'

He said brusquely, 'Thank you for your company at dinner. I'll see you at breakfast.'

'I always have breakfast in my room,' she said calmly. 'I'm not at my best in the mornings.'

'You coped very well with a totally unexpected incident

yesterday morning. I'm sure you'll manage a working breakfast.'

'In that case, of course,' she said in her briskest, most professional tone. 'What time would you like me to be there?' She didn't say sir, but the intimation of the word hung in the air.

'Eight o'clock,' he drawled.

'Then I'll say goodnight.' Gerry tossed him a practised smile and went inside, closing the door behind her with a sharp, savage little push.

But once inside she didn't turn the light on. From a shuttered window, she watched as Bryn Falconer strode along the path between hibiscuses and the elegant bunches of frangipani. Light fell through the slender trunks of the coconuts in lethal silver and black stripes.

He looked so completely at home in these exotic, alien surroundings. It would be easy to imagine him as a sandalwood trader or a pearl entrepreneur two hundred years ago, fighting his way through a region noted for its transcendent beauty and its dangers, taking his pleasures as seriously as he took its perils.

And because that sort of fantasy was altogether too inviting she made herself note the unconscious authority in his face and air and walk. Lord of all he surveyed she thought with an ironic smile.

An intriguing man—and one who was sleeping with Cara.

She shouldn't forget that just because she hated the thought of it. And while she was about it, why not remind herself that although she found him fascinating now, it wouldn't last.

There had been other men. She'd had two serious relationships, and although she'd honestly believed she loved both men, too soon the attraction had died like a flash of tinder without kindling, leaving her with no self-respect.

Because she hated hurting anyone she'd eventually given up on this man-woman thing.

This fiery, dramatic attraction would pass. She just had to keep her head while she waited it out.

CHAPTER FOUR

MORNING in the tropics was always a time of ravishingly
fresh beauty. It would have been perfect if Gerry had been
able to eat her breakfast alone on the small balcony with
its view of the sea.

Nevertheless, she smiled as she showered and dressed.
One of the exasperating things about winter was the extra
clothes needed to keep warm, so she revelled in the freedom of a sundress and light sandals.

Not that she'd skimp on her make-up; painting up like a
warrior going to battle, she thought with a narrow smile as
she opened her cosmetics kit. She'd learned from experts
how to apply that necessary mask so skilfully that even in
the penetrating light of the sun she looked as though she
wore only lip colouring.

And she'd be especially careful now, for reasons she
wasn't prepared to go into. Frowning a little, she smoothed
on tinted moisturiser with sunscreen; and the merest hint
of blusher to give lift and sparkle to her olive skin.

Bryn had made it obvious that this was business, so he'd
get the works—subtle, understated eyeshadow to deepen
the intensity of her dark blue-green eyes, and two shades
of lipstick, carefully applied with a brush and blended, blot-
ted, then applied again.

Grateful that, as well as a tendency to restlessness, her
mother had bequeathed her such excellent skin, Gerry slid
into a gauzy shirt the exact blue of her sundress. She did
not want her shoulders exposed to Bryn Falconer's unset-
tling green gaze.

Sunlight danced through the whispering fronds of the
palms, and close by a dove cooed, a sound that always

lifted her heart. Cynically amused at the anticipation that seethed through her, she picked a frangipani blossom and tucked it into the black curls behind her ear.

In the dining area Bryn rose from a chair as the waitress showed her to his table. Gerry recognised excellent tailoring and the finest cloth in both his trousers and the short-sleeved shirt. Clearly his business paid him very well.

And she'd better stop admiring those wide shoulders and heavily-muscled legs, and collect her wits.

'Good morning,' he said, eyeing her with a definite gleam of appreciation.

'It's a magnificent morning,' she said, squelching the forbidden leap of response as she allowed herself to be seated. 'What happens today?'

'Eat your breakfast first.' He waited a second, then added, 'If you have breakfast.'

She concealed gritted teeth with a false, radiant smile. 'Always,' she returned.

She chose fruit and yoghurt and toast, watching with interest as he ordered a breakfast that would have satisfied a lumberjack.

He looked up, and something in her face must have given her away, because that gleam appeared in his eyes again. 'There's a lot of me to keep going,' he said smoothly.

Unwillingly she laughed. 'How tall are you?'

'Six feet three and a half,' he said, deadpan.

'I thought so. Are your family all as big as you?'

Not a muscle moved in the confident, striking face, but she got the distinct impression of barriers clanging down. 'My mother was medium height. My father was tall,' he said, 'and so was my sister. Tall and big.'

All dead, by the way he spoke.

'You,' he resumed calmly, 'are tall, but very feminine. It's those long, elegant bones.' He paused, his eyes sliding over her startled face. 'And you walk like a breeze across the ocean, like the wind in the palms, graceful and unselfconscious. You don't look as though you know how to make a clumsy movement. Feminine to the core.'

He put his hand beside hers on the table. Emphasised by crisp white linen, the corded muscles of his forearm exuded an aura of efficient forcefulness. In the dappled light of the sun the glowing vermilion and ruby hibiscus flowers in the centre of the table seemed to almost vibrate against his golden-brown skin.

Beside his, her slender fingers, winter-pale, looked both sallow and ineffectual. And out of place.

Gerry gave herself a mental shake. Stop it, she commanded; you're competent enough.

Lean, blunt fingers rested a fraction of a moment on the shadowed veins at her wrist; his touch went through her like fire, like ice, speeding up the pulse that carried its effects in micro-seconds to the furthest part of her body. Drymouthed, a sudden thunder in her ears blocking out the mournful calling of the doves, she quelled an instinctive jerk. Even though he lifted his hand immediately, the skin burnt beneath his touch.

If his plan had been to show her how fragile she was against his strength he'd succeeded, but she saw no reason to let him know.

'Thank you,' she said. Thank heavens her voice didn't betray her. It sounded the same as it always did—cool, a little amused. 'But all women are feminine, you know, just as men are masculine. It goes with the sex.'

And could have bitten her tongue. Why did everything she said to him, everything he said to her, seem imbued with an undercurrent of innuendo, an earthy sensuality that neither of them would acknowledge?

'Some women seem to epitomise it,' he said drily, and glanced up with a smile for the waitress arriving with coffee.

Feeling as though she'd been released from some kind of hypnotic spell, Gerry filled her lungs with fresh, salt-tinged air, and studiously applied herself to getting as much caffeine inside her as she could.

Not that she needed any further stimulus. Her nerves were jumping beneath her skin, and thoughts skittered feverishly through her mind.

Nothing like this, she thought distractedly, had ever happened to her before. Still, although it would be foolish to pretend she was immune to Bryn's dark magnetism, she had enough self-discipline to wait it out. If she deprived this firestorm of fuel, it would devour itself until it collapsed into ashes, freeing her from his spell.

All she had to do was behave with decorum and confidence until it happened. And whenever she felt herself weakening, she'd just recall that he'd slept with Cara.

Yes, that worked; every time Gerry's too-pictorial brain produced images of them in bed together, she felt as though someone had just flung a large bucketful of cold water across her face.

Uncomfortable, but exactly what she needed.

'So what are your plans for this morning?' she asked when her leaping pulses had steadied and she was once more sure of her voice.

'We go for a walk,' he told her.

Gerry allowed her brows to lift slightly. 'A walk?'

'Yes. You do walk, I assume?'

She refused to acknowledge the taunt. 'Naturally,' she said graciously.

'Good. There are only three vehicles on the island.' He smiled. 'Nobody knows who you are, and nobody will expect anything more than a hotel guest's interest in the handicrafts.'

'We're keeping this a secret now?' she asked directly.

'I'd prefer no one to know what you're here for.' He met her gaze with a bland smile that set her teeth on edge.

Shrugging, she looked away. 'You're the boss.'

He was partly right—nobody knew who Gerry was. However, the people they met certainly knew who he was, and they did not view her as a casual hotel guest. They thought she was Bryn Falconer's woman.

He added fuel to their speculation by his attitude, a cool attentiveness that had something possessive about it.

She should have been profoundly irritated. Instead, her body tingled with life, with awareness, with a charged, vital attention, so that even when he was out of her direct sight she knew where he stood, felt him with a sixth sense she'd never experienced before.

Before long she realised the islanders' smiles and open interest meant they approved. The women who sat in groups plaiting the fine fibre greeted Bryn with pleasure and a familiarity that surprised her. Perhaps he was related to them; that would explain his concern.

On the floor of one of a cluster of thatched houses, incongruous beneath corrugated iron roofs, one old woman grinned at Bryn and made a sly comment in the local tongue, a little more guttural than the Maori spoken in New Zealand. He laughed and said something that set her rolling her eyes, but she retorted immediately, her dark eyes flicking from Gerry's set face to Bryn's.

Bryn shot back an answer that had everyone doubling over with mirth. Night school, Gerry decided with a flash of anger; as soon as she got back home she'd register in a Maori conversation class. For years she'd intended to, and now she was definitely going to do it.

'Sorry,' Bryn said, making no attempt to translate.

'That's all right,' she said too sweetly, her smile as polished and deadly as a stiletto. 'I'm a humble employee—it's not for me to show any offence.'

Mockery glinted in his eyes. 'I like a woman who knows her place. Let's go and see how they make the hats.'

As she watched the skilled, infinitely patient fingers weaving fine strands of fibre, Gerry said, 'They do need updating. Are you serious about increasing exports?'

'This is all the islanders have got,' he said. 'They use

the income from the industry to pay for secondary and tertiary education for their children and for health care. Fala'isi provides primary education and a nurse and clinic, but anything else they have to work for themselves. And this is the only export they have.'

'I thought you said they had pearls.'

He shook his head. 'Not here. We're negotiating to set up a pearl industry, but that's a long-term project. The hats are an assured market—if we can keep and expand it.'

'If I sent some photographs, could they copy them?'

Bryn asked the old woman, who was working with two small, almost naked children playing around her feet. Clearly the leader of the group, she frowned and answered at length.

'Yes,' Bryn said, 'they could do that.'

After a round of farewells they left the village behind and walked on beneath the feathery, rustling crowns of coconut palms. The heat collected there, intensifying, thick. Eventually Gerry gave in and eased her shirt off.

Bryn didn't even look at her.

So much, she thought acidly, for not wanting to expose myself. Aloud she said, 'I can find photographs of hats that will sell much better than these. Luckily everyone in the world wants to keep the sun off their face now. But to make it work properly, they need an agent to keep them in contact with what's going on in fashion. There'll always be a small market for the classic styles, but if they want to expand they need someone with a good knowledge of trends.'

Bryn nudged a thin black and white dog out of his way. Fragments of white shell clattered as the dog scrambled up and slouched towards a large-leafed bush. Once in the shade, it gave itself a couple of languid scratches and yawned fastidiously before settling to sleep. Three hens and a rooster clucked amiably by, ignoring the dog, which pricked its ears although it didn't lift its head from its paws.

Gerry laughed softly. 'I'll bet he'd give one of his teeth to chase them.'

'Not if he wants to live. All food is precious here.'

Something oblique in his voice caught her attention. She gave him a sharp sideways glance. 'I suppose it is,' she said, because the silence demanded a response.

'Are you thirsty?' he asked abruptly.

His words suddenly made her aware that her throat was dry. 'Yes, actually I am.'

'Why didn't you say?'

She reacted to the irritation in his voice with a snap. 'There's no shop close by, so what's the use?'

'Dehydrating in this climate can be dangerous. And drinks are all around us. If—' with an intolerable trace of amusement in the words '—you like coconut milk.'

'I do, but I certainly don't want you going up there,' she answered, tipping back her head to eye the bunches of nuts, high above them at the top of the thin, curved trunks.

'It's not dangerous.'

A boy with brilliant dark eyes and a ready smile came swinging through the palms, armed, as many of the children were, with a machete half as tall as he was. After he and Bryn had conducted a cheerful conversation, the boy used a loop of rope to climb the palm with verve and flair. Trying to tell herself he'd probably done it a hundred times before, Gerry watched with anxiety.

'He's an expert,' Bryn reassured her with a smile. 'All the boys here can climb a coconut palm—it's a rite of passage, like learning to kick a football.'

'No doubt, but at least when you play rugby you're on the ground, not a hundred feet above it,' she said, breathing more easily when she saw the boy cut a green nut from the bunch at the crown of the palm and begin swinging down.

Back on the ground, he smiled bashfully at Gerry's thanks, sliced the top off the green nut with a practised flick of the machete, and presented it to her with a gamin grin, before disappearing through the palms towards the beach.

'Mmm, lovely,' Gerry said when she'd drunk half of the clear, refreshing liquid. 'Do you want some?'

She didn't expect Bryn to say yes, but he did, and drank the rest of the liquid down. Strangely embarrassed, she looked away. It seemed such an intimate thing, his mouth where hers had been, the coconut milk going from her lips to his.

You're being stupid, her common sense scolded. Just because he makes your skin prickle, because he has this weird effect on you, you're concocting links. Stop it this minute. Right now. And don't start it again.

'We'd better go back,' Bryn said. 'We've come quite a way and it's starting to get hot.'

On the way back she asked casually, 'When did you learn to speak Maori?'

'I grew up speaking it,' he said drily.

Not exactly a mine of information. Perversely, because it was clear he had no intention of satisfying her curiosity, she pursued, 'You're very fluent.'

'I should be. I lived here until I was ten.'

The depth of her need to know more startled her. It was this which silenced her rather than his brusque answer. Staring through the sinuous grey trunks of the coconut palms to the dazzle of sea beyond, she thought, I'm not going to try to satisfy such a highly suspect curiosity.

'My father,' he said coolly, 'was a beachcomber. It's not a word used much nowadays; I think he felt it had a romantic ring to it.'

Surprised at her sympathy, Gerry said, 'I don't suppose they were particularly good specimens of humanity, but there's a tang of romance to the term.'

'Not for me,' he said. 'He and my mother eloped from New Zealand and eventually made their way to Longopai. They sponged off the islanders until she died having my sister when I was five. After a few months my father drifted on without us, leaving us with a family here. He never came back.'

'That,' she said in a voice few of her friends had heard, 'was unforgivable.'

'Yes.' He looked down at her, eyes as transparent as green glass, but she had the feeling that he wasn't actually seeing her. 'You know what it's like.'

'At least I had a father who loved me,' she said fiercely. 'You were alone.'

'I had my sister. We weren't unhappy; in fact, we probably led a more idyllic life than most children. Our foster family accepted us completely, and we went to school and played and worked with the other kids until I was ten. My mother's parents discovered that we existed, so they sent someone up to collect us and take us back to New Zealand.'

'That would have been a difficult adjustment.'

He was silent for a moment, then said, 'We weren't the easiest of children to deal with, but our grandparents did their best to civilise us.'

'They succeeded,' she said promptly.

His laugh sent a shiver down her spine. 'In all outer respects,' he said. 'But for the first ten years of my life I ran wild. It's not an easy heritage to outgrow.'

It sounded like a warning, yet why should he warn her—and of what?

She asked, 'Was it difficult to adapt to life in New Zealand?'

'I loathed it.' He spoke reflectively, but beneath the smooth surface of his voice Gerry heard raw anger.

'It must have been terrible,' she said quietly.

'They sent me to a prep school to be beaten into shape. Fortunately I have a good brain, and I played rugby well enough to be in the first fifteen.'

A picture of the young boy, dragged away from the only home he'd ever had, pitched into a situation he had no knowledge of or understanding for, transmuted her sympathy into something more primitive—outrage. 'Your sister?'

'Didn't fare so well,' he said roughly. 'As I said, she was

a big girl, nothing dainty about her. She liked to play rugby too, but our grandparents didn't approve of that. In fact, they didn't approve of her at all, especially when she reached adolescence and shot up until she hit six feet.' He surveyed her with hard, unsparing calculation. 'She wasn't like you—she had no inborn style. She was plain, and because she wasn't valued she became clumsy. By the time she was fifteen she was utterly convinced that she was ugly and uncouth and worth nothing.'

Gerry dragged in a deep breath, fighting back the primal fury that coursed through her. 'Your grandparents have a lot to be ashamed of,' she said, thinking of her cousin Anet, another big, tall woman.

But Anet had been born into a family that loved her, and urged her to make the most of her natural athletic ability. After winning a gold medal in the javelin at the Olympics, she'd settled down to married life with a magnificent man who adored her.

Even after three children, the way Lucas Tremaine looked at his wife sent shivers down Gerry's spine. 'Children should be cherished,' she finished curtly.

A car came chugging down the narrow track towards them, if car it could be called. It might have originally been covered in, but consisted now of four wheels, a bonnet and the seats. When the elderly grey-haired driver saw them he slowed down and stopped.

'Message for you, Bryn,' he shouted above the sound of the engine, 'back at the hotel. They want you now.'

Bryn nodded. 'Hop up,' he said to Gerry.

Gerry was sorry the apology for a car had arrived just then. She hadn't satisfied that ravenous curiosity to know more about Bryn, but she understood now why he despised fashion magazines. No doubt his sister had yearned to look like the models in their pages.

What had happened to her? She cast a glance up at Bryn's implacable profile and as swiftly looked away again.

He'd put her so far out of his mind that she might as well not be there.

Trying not to resent his withdrawal, she leapt down when the car halted in front of the high, intricately thatched building that housed the office and the manager's quarters.

'I'll see you at lunchtime,' Bryn said curtly, and strode into the office.

As Gerry walked to her chalet, sticky and slightly salt-glazed, the taste of green coconut milk still faint on her tongue, she decided it didn't take much intuition to guess that he probably owned the hotel. He certainly organised the sale of the hats, and from what he'd said he was the person who was negotiating the pearling project. It was clear that he felt a profound obligation to the islanders who had given his sister her happy, early years.

Gerry admired that.

'Did you get your message?' she asked during lunch, looking up from her salad.

'Yes, thank you.'

She hesitated, then decided to go ahead with the decision she'd made while showering before the meal. 'Now that I've worked out what the problem is with the hats, there's no need for me to stay. It must be costing you a packet for my accommodation.'

'A week,' he said calmly, his eyes very keen as he studied her face. 'You can stay for the week you were hired for. Besides, you haven't seen much of the hat-making industry.'

Made uncomfortable by his concentrated scrutiny, she shrugged. 'Very well,' she said lightly. 'I'll do that tomorrow.'

His smile was narrow and cutting. 'Bored, Geraldine?'

'Not in the least,' she said truthfully. This seething, elemental attraction was about as far removed from boredom as anything could be. And it didn't help that she was terrified he'd notice its uncomfortable physical manifestations—the increased pulse-rate beating in her throat, the heat in her skin, the darkening of her eyes.

If he had noticed, he didn't remark on it. Irony charged his voice as he said, 'After that you can lie in the sun and gild those glorious legs until the week is up.'

'Tanning is no longer fashionable, I'm afraid.' Her smile was syrupy sweet.

Although he didn't rise to the bait, the hooded, predatory gleam of green beneath his lashes sent a sizzle of sensation down the length of her backbone.

She'd leave the day after tomorrow, but because she liked to keep things as smooth and amicable as possible she wasn't going to make a point of it. Bryn was a man accustomed to getting his own way, and she'd always found it simpler not to oppose such people head-on. She just ignored them and did what she wanted to. As a strategy, it usually worked very well.

He insisted she rest in the heat of the day, and because she was surprisingly tired she lay on the chaise longue in her suite and watched the tasselled shadows of the coconut palms on the floor. She did try to read one of the books she'd brought with her, but when her eyelids drifted down she allowed her fantasies to break through the bounds her conscious mind had set on them.

Later, under another cool and reviving shower, she tried to persuade herself that she must have been asleep, because her thoughts had run together and blurred, just like dreams. But they were all of the same man: Bryn Falconer, with his ice-green eyes and hard, strong face, its only softening feature lashes that were long and thick, and curled at the tips.

Gerry's mother had taught her too well that when you fell in love you created mayhem; you left shattered souls behind. Her father had taught her that falling in love meant unhappiness for the rest of your life. He'd taken one look at her mother and wanted her, and when she left him he'd been broken on the wheel of his own passion.

As his daughter grew into a mirror image of the beautiful, flighty, selfish woman who had abandoned them both, he'd warned her about the impact of her beauty. Gerry had seen it herself; men liked her and wanted her without even knowing her, because she had a lovely face and a way of flirting that made them feel wonderful.

So she'd grown up distrusting instant attraction.

Had some cynical fate made sure it had happened to her—a clap of thunder across the sunlit uplands of her life, dark, menacing and too powerful to be ignored?

For a lazy hour she'd lain in the soothing coolness of the trade winds and listened to the waves purring onto the reef, and slipped the leash on her imagination. She'd drowned in the sensuous impact of images of Bryn smiling, talking, of Bryn holding the baby...

Sheer, moony self-indulgence, she thought crossly.

All right, so she was physically attracted to the man— he was sexy enough to be a definite challenge, and that aura of steely power set her nerves jumping and her pulses throbbing—but she wasn't going to get carried away on a tide of imagination and wish herself into disillusion.

Armed with resolution, she went down to the lagoon and swam for twenty minutes in a sea as warm as her bath. She was wringing out her hair as she walked up the beach— swiftly, because the sand burned the soles of her feet— when her skin tightened in a reaction as primitive as it was involuntary.

Tiger-striped by shadow, Bryn stood beneath the palms. His eyes were hidden by sunglasses, and for a moment her heart juddered at his patient, watchful stance. Face bare of cosmetics, she felt like some small animal caught in the sights of a hunter, vulnerable, naked. Her legs suddenly seemed far too long, far too bare, and her bathing suit, sedate and sleek though it was, revealed too much of her body.

He didn't smile, and when he said, 'Hello,' an oblique

note in his voice sent something dark and primitive scudding through her.

'Hello,' she replied, keeping her eyes fixed on her small cache of belongings on the sand only a couple of feet away from him. He looked like some golden god from the days when the world was young, imperious and incredibly, compellingly formidable.

Furious with herself, she forced her shaking legs to walk up to her bag. She grabbed the towel from beneath it, and ran it over her shoulders, then dropped it to pick up a pareu. One swift shake wrapped it around her sarong-fashion. She secured it above her breasts with a knot, and anchored back the wet strands of her hair with two combs.

'Good swim?' His voice was gravelly, as though he'd been asleep.

At least he still wore his shirt. 'Glorious. The water's like silk,' she murmured, banishing images of him sprawled across a bed from her treacherous mind.

'That has to be the most interesting way to wear a length of cotton,' he observed gravely.

'Take your sunglasses off when you say that,' she growled in her best Hollywood cowboy manner.

He removed the sunglasses and stuffed them into his pocket. 'Sorry,' he said, a slow smile lingering as he surveyed her with open appreciation. 'I hope you put sunscreen on.'

She could feel his gaze travel across her shoulders, dip to the delicate skin of her cleavage, the smooth length of her arms. Pinned by that too-intimate survey, she thought confusedly that one of the reasons tanning had been so popular was that, like her cosmetics, it gave the illusion of a second skin; exposed under Bryn's questing scrutiny, she felt vulnerable.

With stiff reserve Gerry said, 'Naturally I take care of my skin.'

He seemed fascinated by the pearls of sea water on her shoulders, each cool bubble falling from her wet hair. One lean finger skimmed the slick surface. Such a light touch, and so swiftly removed, yet she felt it right to the pit of her stomach. Her body shouted *yes,* and melted, collapsed in a wave of heat, of painfully acute recognition.

'Oh, you do that,' he said, his voice a little thicker. 'And very well, too. Your skin's flawless—shimmering and seductive, with a glow like ripe peaches. What Mediterranean ancestor gave you that colouring?'

'My mother left before I had a chance to ask her about her ancestors, but one of them was French,' she said harshly, hearing the uneven crack in her voice with horror.

And she forced herself to step away from the tantalising lure of his closeness, from the primal incitement of his touch. Dry-mouthed, her brain cells too jittery to frame a coherent thought, she blundered on, 'However, that's a nice line. I'm sure Cara liked it.'

Something colder than Saturn's frozen seas flickered within the enigmatic depths of his eyes. 'She'd giggle if I said that to her.'

No doubt, but Cara clearly wasn't too young or unsophisticated to sleep with. Gerry shrugged and turned towards the path to the hotel.

Bryn said coolly, 'She spent the night at my place. Not, however, in my bed.'

Gerry made the mistake of glancing back. 'It's none of my business what Cara—or you—do,' she said, struggling to hold her voice steady in the face of the level, inimical challenge of his gaze and tone.

'Do you believe me?' he asked.

'Is it important that I do?'

He smiled, and his gaze lingered on her mouth. 'Yes,' he said levelly. 'Unfortunately it is.'

CHAPTER FIVE

GERRY hesitated, aware that she was about to step into the unknown, take the first, terrifying stumble over a threshold she'd always evaded before. Every instinct shouted a warning, but even a faint, cautionary memory of her mother, and the damage she'd caused in her pursuit of love, couldn't dampen down the fever-beat of anticipation.

'I do believe you,' she said slowly, her fingers tightening on the knotted cotton at her breast. 'I hope you don't hurt her. Although she thinks she's very sophisticated, she's a baby.'

'She knows she's in no danger from me.'

'That's not the point. She's very attracted to you.'

Frowning, he said abruptly, 'I can't do anything about that.'

If she had any intelligence she'd shut up, but something drove her to say, 'You *are* doing something about it. You're encouraging it.'

Broad shoulders moved in a slight shrug. Coldly, incisively, his eyes as hard as splintered diamonds, he said, 'I met her at a dinner party, saw that she was a little out of her depth, and watched her drink too much. I didn't trust the man hovering around, so I offered her a bed for the night.' He repeated with a dark undertone of aggression, of warning, 'A bed, not *my* bed.'

Gerry's humiliating resentment wasn't appeased. 'I know I shouldn't worry about her,' she said, trying to sound as though she were discussing a purely maternal instinct instead of a fierce, female possessiveness unrecognised in her until she'd met Bryn. 'It's just that she's such a kid in some ways.'

One brow lifted slightly as he said, 'You're also her role model, her idea of everything that's sophisticated and successful.'

'I know,' she said, wishing they could talk about someone other than Cara. 'She'll grow out of it.'

'Oh, I'm sure she will. Hero-worship is an adolescent emotion.' Voices from behind made him say with a caustic flick, 'And here is someone else all ready to worship at the shrine of high fashion.'

It was the Australian family—slightly overweight father, artificial wife and the too-thin daughter with the seeking eyes and vulnerable mouth. Although they were all smiling as they came up, their body language gave them away; they'd been quarrelling.

Gerry tamped down her guilty exasperation at their intrusion.

'Had a good day?' Cosmo asked heartily.

'Lovely, thank you.' Gerry smiled at him and saw his eyelids droop. By now thoroughly irritated, she transferred the smile to his wife and daughter. 'What have you been doing?'

'Swimming,' Narelle said with a little snap.

Lacey eyed Gerry. 'I've been diving,' she offered. 'Did you know that when you go down a bit everything turns blue? Even the fish and the coral? It's nothing like the wildlife documentaries.'

Gerry nodded sympathetically. 'They're specially lighted in the documentaries. Still, the ones close to the surface where the sunlight reaches are gorgeous.'

'It's not the same, though,' Lacey said with glum precision.

'It just shows how careful lighting can glamorise things,' Bryn observed.

Gerry kept her countenance with an effort. 'Exactly,' she said drily.

The younger woman shrugged. 'Oh, well, there's a lot

to look at down there, even if it is all blue. I saw a moray eel.'

Narelle pulled a face. 'Ugh.'

Without looking at her, Gerry said, 'In some places they tame them by feeding them.'

'I wouldn't want to get too close to one.' Lacey shuddered, an involuntary movement that turned into a sudden stumble. She flung out a thin arm and clung for a moment to Gerry, fingers bruising her arm. After a moment she straightened and stepped back, face pasty, her angular body held upright, Gerry guessed, by sheer will-power.

Narelle had been laughing at something Bryn said. She turned now, gave her daughter a swift, irritated glance and said, 'Let's go up and shower. All that lying on the beach is exhausting.'

Lacey's eyes wrung Gerry's heart. Adolescence could be the cruellest time; she herself would have suffered much more if she hadn't had a father who loved her, good friends, aunts who'd listened to her and taught her what to wear, and a plethora of cousins to act as sisters and brothers.

This girl seemed acutely alone, and beneath the prickly outer shell Gerry discerned a kind of numb, stubborn fear. She walked up to the cabañas beside her, talking quietly about nothing much, and slowly a little colour returned to Lacey's face.

An hour later, when they met again in the open-air bar, Gerry was glad to see that Bryn was with the younger woman, and that she was laughing. She had, Gerry realised, the most beautiful eyes—large and grey, and when she was amused they shone beneath thick lashes.

Did she remind Bryn of his sister, who'd been awkward and unhappy? What had happened to her?

Gerry chose a long, soothing glass of lime juice to drink, oddly touched to have Lacey follow suit. Bryn's gaze moved from Lacey's face to Gerry's; she almost flinched at the nameless emotion chilling the crystalline depths.

'So what did you two do today?' Narelle asked flirtatiously.

'Checked out hats,' Bryn said.

'Oh, did you? I saw some in the shop here, but they're hopelessly old-fashioned. Quite resolutely unchic.' She dismissed the subject with a wave of her ringed hand. 'We bought pearls. They're good quality.'

And sure enough, around her throat was a string of golden-black pearls, the clasp highlighted with diamonds.

'They're very pretty,' said Gerry politely, and listened as Narelle told her how much they were worth and how to look after them.

A little later, when Narelle suggested that they eat together, Gerry smiled but said nothing. For a moment it seemed that Bryn might refuse, but after a keen glance at Lacey, silent in loose jeans and a white linen shirt, he agreed.

Gerry enjoyed her usual substantial meal, and wondered as Lacey demolished a much bigger one. In spite of Narelle's protests she even ate dessert.

As they drank coffee in the scented, flower-filled night, Lacey made an excuse and left them. A few moments later Gerry followed her to the restroom, slipping quietly in to the sound of retching.

'Lacey, are you all right?' she asked.

Silence, and then a shocked voice. 'I—ah—think I must have a bug,' Lacey muttered from behind the door.

'I'll get your mother.'

'No!' Water flushed. Loudly Lacey said, 'She's not my mother; she's my stepmother. My mother lives in Perth with her new husband.'

Gerry said, 'You shouldn't have to suffer through a stomach bug; I'm sure the hotel will have medication.'

'I'm all right,' Lacey said sullenly.

But Gerry waited until eventually Lacey opened the door and glowered at her. Then she asked, 'How long have you been throwing up after each meal? Your teeth are still all right, so it can't have been going on for long.'

'What do you mean?' the younger girl demanded belligerently, turning her back to wash out her mouth.

Remorselessly Gerry asked, 'Didn't you know that your teeth will rot? Stomach acid strips the enamel off them.'

Colour burned along the girl's cheekbones. Her hands moved rhythmically against each other in a lather of foam.

Gerry pressed on. 'Does your stepmother know?'

'No,' Lacey blurted. 'And she wouldn't care. All she's ever done is pick at me for being fat and greedy and clumsy.'

'Your father will certainly care.'

Doggedly, Lacey said, 'I should have been like my mother instead of like him.' She eyed Gerry. 'She's tall too.'

I hope to heaven this is the right way to tackle this, Gerry thought. Her hands were damp and tense, but she took a short breath and ploughed on. 'You're never going to be tall. Even if you kill yourself dieting—and that's entirely possible—you'll never look like your mother. She's a racehorse; you're a sturdy pony. Each is beautiful.'

Lacey glared in the mirror at her with open dislike. A stream of water ran across her writhing hands, flooding away the bubbles. 'It's not fair,' she burst out.

Leaning over to turn off the tap, Gerry said, 'Life's not fair, but you're stacking the odds against yourself. If you don't get help, all your potential—all the essential part of you that's been put on earth to make a difference—will be wasted trying to be something you're not.'

'That's easy for you to say!' Lacey flashed. 'You eat like a horse and I'll bet you don't put on a bit of weight.'

Gerry said calmly, 'That's right. But when I was fourteen I was already this tall, and so thin one of my uncles told me I could pass through a wedding ring. I hated it. I towered over everyone in my class, and I was teased unmercifully.'

'I wouldn't mind,' Lacey muttered.

'Do you like being teased?'

The younger woman bit her lip.

Hoping desperately she wasn't making things worse, Gerry went on, 'You have to find some sort of defence against it, but trying to turn yourself into the sort of person an aggressor thinks you should be is knuckling under, giving up your own personality, becoming the slave of their prejudices.'

Lacey frowned. 'It's fashionable to be thin,' she objected.

'In ten years' time the fashion will have changed. It wouldn't surprise me if it swung back to women like you, women with breasts and thighs and hips. Don't you want to get married?'

'Who'd have me?' she snapped, drying her hands without looking at Gerry.

'A man like the actor who was here last time, whose girlfriend caught your father's eye. I'll bet she wasn't skinny and smelling of vomit all the time.'

Lacey's shoulders hunched. 'She had big boobs and too much backside,' she mumbled, 'but she had long legs.'

'Are you sliding into bulimia because you want to attract boys? Because if you are I can tell you now they don't like women who throw up after every meal, whose skin goes pasty and coarse, whose teeth rot, who smell foul and who look like death.'

'Someone said I was fat,' Lacey muttered, a difficult blush blotching her face and neck. 'A boy I like.'

'So you're putting yourself into death row because someone with no manners—an adolescent dork—makes a nasty, untrue remark?' Brutal frankness might work if the girl wasn't too far down the track. Whatever, she couldn't just stand by and do nothing. 'You're letting someone else force you into his mould.'

'I—no. It's not like that.' But Lacey's voice lacked conviction.

'Is that how you'll go through life? Not as an intelligent person, which you are—you showed that the other night— with valuable talents and ideas and gifts, but a tadpole in a flooded creek, tossed every which way by other people's opinions?'

Open-mouthed, Lacey swung around to stare at her. 'A t-tadpole?' She started to laugh. 'A *tadpole*? No, I d-don't want to be a tadpole!'

'Well, that's where you're heading.' Gerry grinned. 'Instead of being a very self-possessed woman, with confidence and control over your own life. If you give up on yourself you risk losing everything that makes you the individual, unique person you are.'

'I wish it was that simple!' But a thoughtful note in Lacey's voice gave Gerry some hope.

'Nothing's ever simple,' she said, thinking of her reluctant, heated attraction to Bryn Falconer.

'I suppose you think I'm stupid,' Lacey said defensively.

'I told you what I think you are—intelligent, aware, with a sly wit that is going to stand you in good stead one day.'

'And fat,' Lacey finished cynically.

Gerry frowned. 'Promise me something.'

'What?'

Gerry chose her words with care. 'Promise me that when you go home you'll see a counsellor or a woman doctor you trust.' *Or I'll tell your parents.* The unspoken words hung in the scented air.

Lacey bit her lip, then blurted, 'If I do, will you write to me?'

'Yes, of course I will.' Gerry said, 'Are you on e-mail? I'll give you my address.' She hooked a tissue from her small bag and scribbled her address and telephone number on it. 'There. Ring me if you need to talk to someone. And, Lacey, you've got the most beautiful eyes.'

Scarlet-faced, the younger girl ducked her head and stammered her thanks.

'Right, let's go,' Gerry said, still worried, but hoping that somehow she'd managed to get through to the girl.

Apart from Bryn, who gave them both a swift, keen glance, no one seemed to have noticed that they'd been gone quite a while; Narelle was trying covertly to place someone on the other side of the room, and Cosmo was looking at his empty glass with the frown of a man who wonders if it would be sensible to have another.

As Gerry picked up her coffee cup Bryn's dark brows drew together into a formidable line and he looked over her head. From behind came a cheerful voice, 'A telephone call for Ms Dacre.'

'Thank you,' she said, taking the portable telephone from the tray and getting back to her feet. She walked across to the edge of the dining area and said, 'Yes.'

'Gerry, oh, thank God you're there, it's Cara.'

'What's happened?'

'M-Maddie—Maddie Hopkinson—is in hospital.'

Maddie, an extremely popular model who'd come back to New Zealand after three years based in New York, was to have left for Thailand for a shoot the day after next. An important shoot—the start of a huge, Pacific-wide campaign. She'd been through a difficult period, getting over the American boyfriend who'd dumped her when she insisted on coming home, but over the past month or so she seemed to have recovered her old fire and sparkle.

Icy tendrils unfolded through Gerry's stomach. 'In *hospital*? What's the matter with her?'

'She OD'd.' Cara sounded scared.

'*What?*'

'Drugs—her flatmate thinks it might have been heroin.'

Gerry had worried about Maddie, talked to her, suggested counselling, but had never suspected the model was taking drugs. Glancing automatically at her watch—silly, because Langopai was in the same time zone as New Zealand, so it was eight o'clock there too—she asked, 'When was this?'

'Last night.' Cara hesitated, then said in a voice that had horror and avidity nicely blended, 'Sally—the girl she shares a flat with—rang me this morning. Gerry, I went to see her this afternoon—there were police at her door and they wouldn't let me in.'

Shock stopped Gerry's brain. She drew in a deep breath and forced the cogs to engage again, logic to take over from panic. 'Why hasn't Honor contacted me?'

'Because she doesn't know anything about it,' Cara said. 'I've been ringing and ringing her flat, but all I get is the answer-machine. And it's Queen's Birthday weekend, so she won't be back until Tuesday.'

Blast Honor and her habit of taking off for weekends without letting anyone know where she was! Striving very hard to sound calm and in control, Gerry said, 'All right, I'll get a plane out of here as soon as I can. In the meantime, look in my work diary and get me the phone number of—' Her mind went blank. 'Maddie's booker.' The bookers at the agency organised each model's professional appointments.

'Jill,' Cara said. 'All right, I'll be back in a moment.'

While Cara raced off to get her diary from her bedroom Gerry gnawed on her lip and tried to work out what to do next. From the eight or nine guests enjoying the ambience of the communal area came a low, subdued hum of conversation punctuated with laughter. Lights glowed, dim enough to give the soft flattery of candles; she noted with an expert's eye the line and drape of extremely expensive resort wear, the glimmer of pearls, the sheen of pampered skin, the white flash of teeth.

Hurry up, Cara! And hang in there, Maddie, she mentally adjured, thinking of the exquisite, fragile girl lying in her hospital bed with a police guard at the door. Lately there had been a lot of publicity about heroin being chic amongst models and photographers. Oh, why hadn't she noticed something was wrong?

And how would this affect the agency? Her head

throbbed, and she had to take another deep breath. Swinging away to look out over the lush foliage beyond the public area, she scrabbled in her evening bag and found a ballpoint pen.

'I've got it.' Cara's voice wobbled, then firmed. 'Here's Jill's number.' She read it off.

Gerry wrote it on another tissue. 'OK.' She gave Cara the name of the advertising agency in charge of Maddie's shoot. 'Get me the art director's number—it's there.'

'She won't be at work now,' Cara said. 'It's Friday night.'

'She might be. Her home number's there as well, so get it too.'

'Gosh, you're so organised.' Sounds of scrabbling came through the static, until Cara said in a relieved voice, 'Yes, here they are.'

'Let's hope to heaven she either works late or stays home on a Friday night.' Gerry spread out the tissue and began to copy the numbers down as Cara read them out.

When the younger woman had finished she said, 'Gerry, it took me ages to get through to you so you might have trouble ringing New Zealand. Do you want me to ring Jill and tell her what's happened?'

Gerry hesitated. 'Good thinking. And if I haven't got hold of her, ask her to track down the art director and tell her that I suggest Belinda Hargreaves to take Maddie's place. I know she was second choice, and if I remember right she hasn't got anything on at the moment. Jill's her booker too, so she'll know.'

'What if the ad agency or the client doesn't want Belinda?'

Gerry said, 'I'll deal with it when I get back. Don't worry. Many thanks for ringing me. Cara, how is Maddie?'

'She's alive, but that's all I've been able to find out. The hospital won't tell me anything because I'm not a relation, and apparently her brother is still on his way back from Turkestan or somewhere.'

Gerry twisted a curl tight around one finger. Pushing guilt to the back of her mind, she said, 'Send her flowers from us all. And get me the number of the hospital, will you?'

Where the *hell* was Honor? Probably spending the weekend with a man; she had a cheerful, openly predatory attitude where the other sex were concerned, swanning unscathed through situations that would have scared Gerry white-haired.

Why couldn't she have waited until Gerry got back before going off like this? And why, when she knew Gerry would be away, hadn't she left a contact number?

But of course she hadn't known that Gerry was coming up to Longopai. Clearly she'd believed that if anything needed attending to, Gerry would do so, even though she was on holiday.

After soothing Cara some more, Gerry said goodbye, dropped the telephone at the main desk and organised to pay for all phone bills with her credit card, then went back to the table, composing her expression into blandness.

'Problems?' Bryn said, getting to his feet. The ice-green gaze rested on her face, expressionless, measuring.

Damn, how did he know? 'I have to make a few calls,' she said lightly, avoiding a direct answer.

It was none of his business, and she refused to give him a chance to make more comments about her agency exploiting young women. She was feeling bad enough about Lacey and Maddie. Summoning her best smile, she said to the table at large, 'If you'll excuse me, I'll leave you now.'

'That's all right,' Cosmo said breezily. 'See you tomorrow, then.'

She smiled and said goodnight, startled when Bryn said, 'I'll walk you up to your cabaña.'

After a moment's silence she said, 'Thank you.'

He took her arm in a grip that had something both predatory and possessive about it. Back erect, head held high, she smiled at the Australian family and went with him.

When they were out of earshot he said, 'What problem?'

Steadily she said into the sleepy heat of the night, 'I'm sorry, I can't tell you. It's important and urgent—I need to get back to New Zealand as soon as possible.'

'Someone ill?' His voice was cool.

She dithered. 'I—no, I don't think so. I'm needed back at the agency—there's an emergency. I'm sorry about the hats—but I do know now what the problem is, and I'll send you recommendations. If that's not enough, I will, of course, repay the money you've spent—'

'Don't be an idiot.' Although his voice was crisp and scornful, he continued, 'If you have to go, you have to go.'

Surprised that he didn't try to hold her to their agreement, she asked, 'Is there any chance of leaving the island tonight?'

'No,' he said abruptly. 'The seaplane's not authorised for night flights.'

Stopping, she said, 'I'll see if the desk clerk can organise a seat for me on the first flight tomorrow.'

'I'll do it,' he said, urging her on. 'And get you onto a flight out of Fala'isi tomorrow.'

He was being kind, but something drove her to say, 'I can't put you to all that trouble.'

'I have more pull here than you,' he said coolly.

There was no sensible reason why she shouldn't accept his help. Struggling with an inconvenient wariness, she said, 'Thanks. I'd be very grateful.'

'What's happened?'

Gerry resisted the temptation to tell him everything and let him take over. So this, she thought, trying for her usual pragmatism, is the effect a pair of broad shoulders and an air of competence have on susceptible women. Odd that she, who prided herself on being capable and practical and the exact opposite of susceptible, should want to succumb like a wilting Victorian miss.

'Just some trouble at the agency. It's nothing you can help with,' she said woodenly, 'but thank you for offering.'

'You don't know what I can help with.'

Beneath the smooth, amused surface of his voice a note of determination alerted her senses. 'I do know you can't do anything about this,' she said.

He left it at that, although she thought she could sense irritation simmering in him. 'I'll organise your flights to New Zealand and be back in half an hour,' he said.

'Thank you very much.' She made the mistake of glancing upwards. In the soft starlit darkness his face was a harsh sculpture, all tough, forceful power. Sensation slithered the length of her spine, melting a hitherto inviolate impregnability.

It would be easy to want this man rather desperately— so easy, and so incredibly perilous. He was no ordinary man; her cousin Anet's husband had something of the same sort of hard, contained intensity.

No, that was silly. Lucas had fought in a vicious and bloody guerrilla war; he wrote books about conspiracies and events that shook the world. Bryn was an importer. A successful businessman could have nothing in common with a man like Lucas.

After she'd closed the door behind her she exhaled soundlessly. It had been surprisingly difficult to turn down Bryn's offer of a listening ear. He hadn't liked it—no doubt he was accustomed to being the person everyone relied on.

Gerry had never relied on a man in her life, and she wasn't going to start now.

With a swift shake of her head she dialled the hospital, who would only tell her that Maddie was as well as could be expected. After thanking the impersonal voice, Gerry hung up and began damage control.

Jill, the booker who managed Maddie's professional life, already knew of Maddie's illness—although not, Gerry deduced, its nature—and was doing her best to tidy up the situation; she agreed that Belinda was the best replacement they could offer, and had already got in touch with her. Belinda was ready to go.

'Oh, that's great,' Gerry said, breathing a little more easily. 'Now I have to convince the art director at the ad agency that Belinda can do it.'

'I could do that,' Jill said.

'I'm going to have to crawl a bit—it should be me. Still, if you don't hear from me within the hour, start ringing her.'

'Will do. What are her numbers?'

'Bless you,' Gerry said, and told her. Hanging up, she breathed a harassed sigh.

It wasn't going to be easy.

After a frustrating and infuriating twenty minutes she gave up trying to contact the art director, who didn't even have an answering machine. It was useless to keep trying; she needed a good night's sleep, so she'd try again the next morning. And if she still couldn't get her, Jill would.

Swiftly, efficiently, she began to pack.

Half an hour to the minute later there was a knock on the door. Bracing herself, she opened it.

Bryn said, 'I've booked you on a flight from Fala'isi at six o'clock tomorrow morning.'

'But the seaplane—'

'I'll take the cabin cruiser and get you to Fala'isi before then.' His gaze took in her suitcase. 'Good, you're ready. Let's go.'

Taken aback, she protested, 'But—'

He interrupted crisply, 'I thought you wanted to get back to New Zealand in a hurry?'

'Yes! I—well, yes, of course I do.' Yet still she hesitated. 'I presume you know how to get from here to Fala'isi in a strange cabin cruiser?'

His mouth curved. 'The cruiser's mine. And with radar and all the modern aids, navigation's like falling off a log. Besides, I do know these waters—I come up here quite often.'

Feeling stupid, she said, 'Well—thank you very much.'

He lifted her case and she went with him through the

palms, past the public area, out onto the clinging, coarse white coral sand of the beach, where the hotel's outrigger canoe was ready. The two men who'd picked her up from the plane were there; they said something in the local Maori to Bryn, who answered with a laugh, and before long they were heading across the lagoon, the only sound a soft hissing as the hulls sliced through the black water.

Gerry had a moment of disassociation, a stretched fragment of time when she wondered what she was doing there beneath stars so big and trembling and close she felt she could pick them like flowers. The scents of sea and land mingled, the fresh fecundity of tropical vegetation balanced by the cool, salty perfume of the lagoon.

Thoughts spun around her brain, jostling for their moment in the light, then sliding away into oblivion. She should be trying to work out how to help Maddie. Bryn would be disgusted if he knew; poor Maddie's condition would be another nail in Gerry's coffin, another thing to despise her for.

Was he right? Was her career one that drove young women down Lacey's path? Would Maddie have begun using heroin if she hadn't been a model? Would Lacey be bulimic if she hadn't longed to be thin?

Stricken, she pushed the thoughts to the back of her brain and looked around.

The starlit silence, the swift flight of the canoe, the noiseless islanders and the awe-inspiring beauty of the night played tricks on her mind. She wondered if this was what it would be like to embark on a quest into the unknown, a quest from which she'd return irrevocably transformed. Her eyes clung to Bryn's profile, arrogant against the luminous sky. Something tightened into an ache inside her; swallowing, she looked hastily away.

You've been reading too much mythology, she told herself caustically. What you're doing is catching a plane home to Maddie's personal tragedy, and there's nothing remotely magical about that!

Paddles flashed, slowing the canoe's headlong flight; carefully, precisely, they eased up to the white hull of the cruiser. Bryn stood up, and in one lithe movement hauled himself up and over the railing. Within two minutes he'd unzipped the awning and lowered steps from the cockpit. Gerry climbed up and waited while Bryn stooped to take her case from the hands of one of the men.

'Thank you,' she said.

They smiled and waved and sped off into the darkness.

CHAPTER SIX

FEELING oddly bereft, Gerry said, 'What happens now?'

Bryn gestured at a ladder and said, 'I'm going up to the flybridge because I can see better from up there. You might find it interesting to watch as we go out.'

'Can I do something?'

'No.'

The surprisingly large flybridge was roofed in and furnished with comfortable built-in sofas. One faced a bank of intimidating gauges and switches and dials beneath what would have been the windscreen in a car. There was even, Gerry noted, what appeared to be a small television screen. The other sofa was back to back with the first, so that it faced the rear of the boat where awnings blocked out the night. There was enough seating for half a dozen people.

Without looking at her, Bryn sat down in front of the console and began to do things. The engine roared into life and small lights sprang into action.

Wishing that she knew more about boats, Gerry perched a little distance from him and wrinkled her nose at the hot, musty air. Presumably the awnings at the back were usually raised—lowered? removed?—while the boat was in use.

As though she'd spoken, Bryn pressed a button and two of the side awnings slid to one side, letting in a rush of fresh air.

Desperately worried though she was about Maddie, Gerry couldn't entirely squelch a humiliating anticipation. A lazy inner voice that came from nowhere, all purring seductiveness, murmured, Oh, why worry? A few moments of fantasy can't do any harm.

Turning his head, Bryn asked, 'Will you hold her steady

while I haul up the anchor? Keep her bow pointed at the clump of palms on the very tip of the outer passage. You won't have to do anything more than that, and it's so calm you won't have any trouble.'

Her stomach lurched slightly, but he made the request so casually that she said, 'Fine,' and got to her feet, gripping the wheel tightly while he disappeared. She stared at the graceful curves of the palms until her eyes started to blur. She rested them by watching Bryn down on the deck in front.

He began to haul on the anchor chain, bending into the task with a strength that sent an odd little flutter through her. Broad shoulders moving in a rhythm as old as time, he pulled with smooth precision, power and litheness combining in a purely masculine grace.

He'd be a magnificent lover, prompted that sly inner voice.

A sudden rattle, combined with the stirring wheel in her hands, persuaded her to shut off the tempting images conjured by that reckless inner voice. Guiltily she looked back at the palm trees, breathing her relief that the bow still pointed in the right direction

'Good work,' Bryn said, coming up noiselessly beside her and taking over. 'Are you tired?'

'A bit.' She moved aside to gaze out across the water, smooth and dark as obsidian, polished by the soft sheen of the tropical stars. Heat gathered in her veins, seeping through her like warmed honey. She felt like a woman from the dawn of time, aware yet unknowing, standing on the edge of the first great leap into knowledge. 'It's a wonderful night.'

'Tropical nights are known for their seductive qualities,' Bryn agreed, his voice pleasant and detached.

It sounded like a warning. Gerry kept her gaze fixed on the lagoon. 'I'm sure they are,' she said drily.

'But you don't find them so.'

She shrugged. 'They're very beautiful. So is a summer's night at home—or a winter's one, for that matter.'

'A dyed-in-the-wool New Zealander,' he jibed.

'Afraid so. I think if you've been happy in a place you'll always love it.'

'And in spite of growing up motherless you were a happy child?'

'I was lucky,' she said. 'I had innumerable relations who treated me like their own child. And my father was very devoted.'

'His death must have hit you hard,' he said, looking down at the instruments behind the wheel.

'Yes.' Four years previously her father's heart had finally given up the struggle against the punishing workload he'd been forced to take on in his retirement years.

'I liked him,' Bryn said.

Gerry nodded, not surprised that they had met. New Zealand was small, and most people in a particular field knew everyone in it. Her father had earned his position as one of New Zealand's most far-sighted businessmen, building up his small publishing business into a Pacific Rim success.

She'd mourned her father and was over his death—or as over it as she'd ever be—but because the memory still hurt she asked, 'Did you ever try to find out what happened to *your* father?'

If he snubbed her, she wouldn't blame him.

But he answered readily enough, although a stony undernote hardened his words. 'He'd been hired as crew on a yacht headed for Easter Island. He died there in an accident.'

'A lonely place,' she said, thinking of the tiny, isolated island, the last outpost of Polynesia, so far across the vast Pacific that it was ruled from South America.

'Perhaps that's what he wanted. Loneliness, oblivion.' His voice was coolly objective. 'He didn't even have a headstone.'

For some reason the calm statement wrung Gerry's heart.
'Have you been there?'

'A year ago.'

She stared at the white bow wave chuckling past. 'Did
you find anyone who knew him?'

'Several remembered what had happened. Apparently he
got drunk and set out to swim ashore. He was washed up
on the beach the following day. I tried to trace the yacht,
but to all intents and purposes it sailed over the edge of the
world. It certainly didn't turn up in any of the registers after
that.'

At least she had been loved and valued! Tentatively she
asked, 'He must have been shattered by your mother's
death. Do you remember him?'

'Only that he was a big man with a quick, eager laugh.
The islanders called him a starchaser, because you can
never catch a star.'

'Like my mother,' she said softly, warmed by a sense of
kinship. 'I don't know whether she ever knew what she
wanted, but she certainly never got it.'

'Damaged people, perhaps. Both of them unable to accept responsibility for themselves or their children.'

Gerry nodded, watching as the bow swung, steadied,
headed towards the black gap in the reef that was the channel. 'That passage looked very narrow from the air. Is it
difficult to take a boat through?'

'Not this one. Longopai's trading vessel has to stand off
and load and unload via smaller boats, but a craft this size
has no trouble.' She looked up and saw a corner of his
mouth lift, then compress. He went on, 'I know the channel
as well as I know the way I shave. Besides, with the equip-
ment on the *Starchaser* it would take an act of God or sheer
stupidity to get us into any sort of trouble. Relax.'

Why had he called his boat after his father? Some sort
of link to the man who'd abandoned him and his sister—
or a warning? A glance at his profile, all hard authority in
the greenish light of the dials and screens, destroyed that

idea. No hint of sentiment or whimsy in those harsh male angles and lines. A warning, then.

Aloud, Gerry said lightly, 'I trust you and the *Starchaser*'s instruments entirely.'

He sent her a sharp glance before saying equivocally, 'Good.'

Nevertheless she didn't distract him with conversation while he took the cruiser through the gap, admiring the efficient skill with which he managed the craft in a very narrow passage. Once through, the boat settled into a regular, rocking motion against the waves.

'I forgot to ask,' Bryn said. 'Do you get seasick?'

'I haven't ever done so before.'

'There's medication down in the head if you need it.'

'The head?' she asked, smiling.

He turned the wheel slightly. In an amused voice he said, 'The bathroom. There are three on board, one off each of the staterooms and another for the other cabins.'

'Such opulence,' she said lightly.

'Never been on a luxury cruiser before?' he asked, the words underlined with a taunt.

'Quite often,' she said, then added, 'But always as a mere day passenger. And for some reason I assumed that luxury didn't mean much to you.'

He shrugged. 'I like comfort as much as the next man,' he said. 'But I can do without it. The boat is used mostly by guests from the hotel, and as they're brought here by the promise of luxury—and pay highly for it—the boat has to follow suit. There's no luxury at all on Longopai's trading vessel.'

'Does the vessel belong to the islanders?'

'Yes. They had no regular contact with the rest of the world. The trader has made quite a difference for them.'

Had he bought it for them?

Somewhere to the south lay Fala'isi, lost for now in the darkness. With a throb of dismay Gerry thought that she could stand like this for the rest of her life, watching the stars wheel slowly overhead in a sky of blue-black immensity, and listening to Bryn.

As soon as she realised where it was leading, she banished the delusion.

She was not, she told herself sternly, falling even the tiniest bit in love with Bryn Falconer. 'Do you know Lacey's address?' she asked, filling in a silence that was beginning to stretch too long.

'I could find out. Why?'

'I want to send her a photograph of my cousin and her husband,' she said. 'Anet threw the javelin for an Olympic gold; she's as tall as me and about three sizes bigger—a splendid Amazon of a woman.'

'Anet Carruthers? I saw her win. She threw brilliantly.'

'Didn't she just! One of my most exciting experiences was watching her get the gold. Her husband is gorgeous, and I think it might cheer Lacey up if she could see them together.'

'You continually surprise me,' he said after a moment.

'People who make incorrect assumptions based solely on physical appearance must live in a state of perpetual astonishment,' she returned evenly.

He laughed quietly. 'How right you are. I'm sorry.'

'You judged me without knowing anything about me,' she said, the words a crisp reprimand.

'Admitted. First appearances can be deceiving.'

When he strode into her house Gerry had thought him a hard man, exciting and different and far too old for Cara. Certainly she'd not suspected him to be capable of tenderness for a baby, or such kindness as this trip to Fala'isi. A little ashamed, she said, 'Well, anyone can make a mistake.'

She fought back a bewildering need to ask him more about his life, find out who his friends were and whether they shared any. Pressing her lips firmly together, she forced herself to think of other, far more urgent matters.

How was Maddie? And why—*why*—did someone with her advantages throw everything away in servitude to a drug?

When she recovered—Gerry refused to think she might not—they'd do their best for her, see that she got whatever help she needed to pull her life together. Honor would know what to do; she'd spent four years with a heroin-addicted lover. In the end she'd escaped with nothing but her dream of opening a modelling agency.

Frowning, Gerry wondered again whether Bryn was right. Did the constant pressure of unrealistic expectations lead young women into eating disorders and drug abuse?

She hugged her arms around her, turning slightly so that she could see the face of the man silhouetted against the soft glow of the instrument panels; as well as the powerful contours, the faint light picked out the surprisingly beautiful, sensuous curve of his mouth.

Something clutched at her nerves, dissolved the shield of her control, twisted her emotions ever tighter on the rack of hunger. For the first time in her life she felt the keen ache of unfulfilled desire, a needle of hunger and frustration that stripped her composure from her and forced her to accept her capacity for passion and surrender.

Hair lifted on the back of her neck. This was terrifying; she had changed overnight, altered at some deep cellular level, and she'd never be the same again.

'Why don't you go on down and sleep?'

Bryn's voice startled her. Had he noticed? No, how could he? 'I think I will,' she returned.

'The bed in the starboard cabin won't be made up, but the sheets are in the locker beside the door.'

'Is starboard left or right? I can never remember.'

'Right,' he said. Amused, he continued, 'Starboard and right are the longer words of each pair—port and left the shorter.'

'Thanks. Goodnight, Bryn. And thank you. This is wonderfully kind of you.'

'It's nothing.' He sounded detached.

Rebuffed, she made her way down to the cockpit, and then down three more steps to the main cabin. At the end a narrow door opened into an extremely comfortable little cabin, with a large double bed taking up most of the floor space. Close by, her suitcase rested on a built-in bench beneath a curtained band of windows.

After making the bed and discovering the secrets of the tiny *en suite*—only here it was a head, she reminded herself—Gerry slipped off her shoes and lay down. Soon this would be over. She'd fly back to New Zealand, and after that she'd make sure she didn't see much of Bryn. He was too dangerous to her peace, too much of a threat. And banishing the treacherous little thought that he'd never bore her, she courted sleep.

She woke to the gentle rocking of the boat, a bar of sunlight dazzling her closed eyes. For several moments she lay smiling, still mesmerised by dreams she no longer remembered, and then as her eyes opened and she stared through the gap in the curtains she gasped and shot upright.

Daylight here was just after six, so by now she should be high on a jet, heading back to New Zealand. A startled glance at her watch revealed that it was nine minutes past eight. No, she should be landing in the cold grey winter of Auckland. Jolted, she leapt off the bed and ran from the cabin.

Bryn was stretched out on a sofa, but his eyes were open, densely green and shadowed in his grim face. As Gerry skidded to a halt and demanded breathlessly, 'What's going on? Why are we stopped?' he got up, all six feet three and a half of him.

Tawny hair flopped over his forehead; raking it back, he said, 'The bloody electronics died, so I can't get the boat to go—or contact anyone.'

Her stomach dropped. Taking a short, involuntary step backwards she asked, 'Where are we?'

'I used the outboard from the inflatable to get us inside

a lagoon, so we're safe enough, but it won't take us to Fala'isi.'

A swift glance revealed that they were anchored off a low, picture-postcard atoll. Blinking at a half-moon of incandescent white sand, Gerry concentrated on calming her voice to its usual tone and speed. 'Can the islanders get us to Fala'isi? It's really important that I get back as soon as I can.'

'There are no islanders.' At her blank stare he elaborated. 'It's an uninhabited atoll about a hectare in extent.'

'Flares,' she urged. 'Distress flares—haven't you got any?'

'Five. I plan to fire them if we hear a plane or see a boat. It's our best chance of being found.'

'You don't sound very hopeful,' she said tautly.

Wide shoulders moved in the slightest of shrugs. 'The plane to Longopai flies the shortest route, and we're well off his track, but if he's looking in the right place at the right time he'll see a flare. The same goes for boats.'

While she stood there, scrabbling futilely for a solution, he asked without emphasis, 'Why is it so important for you to get back?'

'There's a problem with the agency,' she evaded woodenly.

'Surely you have someone in charge while you're away?'

'Honor McKenzie—my partner—but they can't get hold of her.'

He frowned. 'Why?'

'She's gone away without leaving a contact number,' Gerry snapped.

'Is that usual?'

She moved edgily across to the window, staring out. The boat rocked in the small waves; somewhere out there a fringing reef tamed the huge Pacific rollers. On the atoll, three coconut palms displayed themselves like a poster for a travel agency, and several birds flashed silver in the sun as they wheeled above the vivid waters of the lagoon. The sky glowed with the rich, heated promise of a tropical day.

It's not the end of the world, she told herself, taking three deep breaths. Even if I don't get back today or tomorrow it's not the end of the world. Jill will contact that wretched art director at the ad agency, and organise Maddie's replacement—the bookers know their stuff so well they can function without Honor.

Even if the art director or the client throws a tantrum and refuses to use Belinda, *it's still not the end of the world.*

But her body knew better. The last—the very last!— thing she wanted to do was spend any time shut up in a boat—however luxurious—with Bryn Falconer. An hour was too much.

Stomach churning, she said, 'Every so often Honor likes to get away from everything.'

'When you're not there?'

The dark voice sounded barely interested, yet a whisper of caution chilled her skin.

'She'll probably be back on Tuesday, but I need to get back *now*.' Her voice quavered. Gamely, she snatched back control and, because anything seemed better than letting him know that she was acutely attracted to him and terrified of it, she added, 'One of our models is ill, and there are things to be organised. I told Cara I'd be back today. She'll worry.' Quickly, before he had a chance to probe further, she asked, 'How on earth could everything fail on the boat? Surely the engine isn't run by electronics?'

'I'm afraid that it is,' he said. 'Just like your car—if the computer dies, it won't go.'

'Why can't you fix it? You're supposed to be an expert on computers, aren't you?' Shocked outrage shimmered through her voice, putting her at a complete disadvantage.

'Geraldine, I import them,' he said, as though explaining something to a child. 'I don't make them, and when my computers go down I call in professionals to fix them. I'm sorry, but I can't find out what the problem is.'

'So that means we have no facilities—we're not able to cook—'

'Calm down,' he said easily. 'The kitchen and heads are powered by gas. There's a small auxiliary engine that I can use to charge the generator with, so we'll have light. You're not going to be living in squalor, Geraldine.'

The taunting undernote irked her, but she ignored it. 'Can't you use that other engine to fix the electronic system? No, that wouldn't work.'

'Electronic systems don't run on fossil fuels,' he agreed tolerantly. 'Besides, the fault is in the electronics themselves, not the power.'

She cast a glance at his face with its shadow of beard. Although he didn't look tired, he might have been up all night getting them to safety. Dragging in another breath, she asked more moderately, 'How long do you think we'll have to wait here?'

His eyes were hooded and unreadable. 'I have no idea. Until someone comes looking for us.'

'When will they miss you?'

'They won't,' he told her. 'The islanders are accustomed to me taking off whenever I feel like it. But if you told Cara you'd be back today I'd say it will be tonight or tomorrow.'

Relief flooded her. 'Yes,' she said slowly. 'Yes, of course.'

'As soon as you don't turn up she'll alert people, and we'll be found.'

Gerry sank down onto the leather sofa. 'I'm sorry,' she said after a moment. 'I don't usually fly off the handle like that.'

'Everyone involved in a shipwreck is entitled to a qualm or two.'

Damn him, his mouth quirked. She bared her teeth in what she hoped looked like a smile. 'I suppose it is a shipwreck,' she said. 'On a desert island, of all places. How fortunate there are no pirates nowadays.'

'The world is full of pirates,' he said. His tone was not exactly reassuring, and neither were his words.

Gerry stared at him. 'What do you mean?' she asked uncertainly.

'Just that there are people around who would steal from you,' he said. 'If for any reason I'm not on board, be careful who you let in. Not that you're likely to have to face such a situation, but Fala'isi—and Longopai too—have their share of unpleasant opportunists.'

If that was meant to be reassuring, he should take lessons. A stress headache began to niggle behind one eye. Straining for her usual calm pragmatism, she said, 'Then I hope we get away before the local variety turns up. I have to tell you that although it sounds really romantic, being stranded has never appealed to me. And a steady diet of fish and coconuts will soon get boring.'

'There are staples on board,' he said casually. 'Plenty of water and tinned stuff. With fish and coconuts we have enough for a couple of weeks.'

'A couple of weeks!' she repeated numbly.

'Cheer up, we won't be here for that long. Would you like some breakfast?'

Gerry suddenly realised that she was still wearing the crumpled clothes she'd slept in. Worse, she hadn't combed her hair or cleaned her teeth.

Or put any make-up on.

Abruptly turning back to her cabin, she said, 'Thanks—just toast, if we've got bread. And coffee. I'll go and tidy up first.'

In the luxurious little bathroom Gerry peered at herself in the mirror, hissing when she saw a riot of black hair around her face, and eyes that were three times too big, the pupils dilated enough to make her look wild and feverish. Hastily she washed and got into clean clothes before reducing her mop to order and putting on her cosmetics.

When at last she emerged Bryn was making toast in the neat kitchen. A golden papaya lay quartered on the bench, its jetty seeds scooped from the melting flesh. Beside a hand of tiny, green-flecked bananas stood a bowl of oranges and the huge green oval of a soursop.

'Where did you get all this?' she asked.

'No sensible person travels by sea without loading some food,' he said evenly. 'It's a huge ocean, and every year people die in it, some from starvation. How many pieces of toast do you want?'

'Only a couple, thanks. I'm not very hungry.'

'You have a good appetite for someone so elegant.'

Sternly repressing a forbidden thrill of pleasure at the off-hand compliment, Gerry said, 'Thank you. Perhaps.'

He gave her a narrow glance, then smiled, reducing her to mindlessness with swift, intensely sexual charm. 'You're right,' he said blandly. 'Commenting on someone's appetite is crass. And you must know that you're not just elegant; you have the sort of beauty that takes the breath away.'

Shaken by her clamouring, unhindered response, Gerry said unevenly, 'From one extreme to the other. You're exaggerating—but thank you.'

'There should be a tablecloth in the narrow locker by the table,' Bryn told her. 'Plates and cutlery in the drawers beside it.'

Still quivering inside, she set the table, using the familiar process to regain some equilibrium.

By the time she sat down to fruit and toast she'd managed to impose an overlay of composure onto her riotous emotions. To her surprise she was hungry—and that bubble in her stomach, that golden haze suffusing her emotions was expectation.

Worried by this insight, she looked down at the table. In the morning sunlight the stainless steel knives and forks gleamed, and she'd never noticed before how pristine china looked against crisp blue and white checks, or how clean and satisfying the scents of food and coffee were.

Bryn was wearing a pale green knit polo shirt that emphasised the colour of his eyes and his tanned skin. He looked big and dangerous and powerfully attractive. Fire ran through her veins; resisting it, she forced herself to butter her toast, to spread marmalade and to drink coffee.

'I'll clean up in the kitchen if you want to go and fiddle with the electronics,' she offered when the meal was over.

'Sea-going vessels don't have kitchens.' He sounded amused. 'You come from the country with the biggest number of boats per person in the world, and you don't know that a boat's kitchen is called a galley?'

She shrugged. 'Why should I? My family ski and play golf in the winter, and play polo and tennis and croquet in the summer.'

'I'm not surprised,' he said, and although there was almost no inflection in his voice she knew it wasn't a compliment.

Smiling, each word sharpened with the hint of a taunt, she returned, 'All the yuppie pastimes.'

'But your family aren't yuppies,' he drawled. 'They're the genuine twenty-four-carat gold article, born into the purple.'

'Hardly. Emperors of Byzantium we're not!'

'No, just rich and aristocratic for generations.'

She lifted her brows, met gleaming eyes and a mouth that was hard and straight and controlled. Some risky impulse persuaded her to say, 'Do I detect the faint hint of an inferiority complex? But why? If your grandparents sent you to a private school they had money and social aspirations.'

The moment the words left her mouth she wished she'd kept silent. Instinct, stark and peremptory, warned her that this man didn't take lightly to being taunted.

'My maternal ones did. The other two lived in a state house with no fence and no garden, and a couple of old cars almost buried in grass on the lawn.' His voice betrayed nothing but a cool, slightly contemptuous amusement. 'Don't worry, Geraldine, I won't tell your family and friends that you've been slumming it.'

Damn, she'd hit a nerve with her clever remark. Beneath the surface of his words she sensed jagged, painful rocks...

Stacking her coffee mug onto her bread-and-butter plate, she said, 'I'm not a snob. Like most New Zealanders with any intelligence, I take people as I find them.'

'And how do you find me?'

Something about the way he spoke sent slow shivers along her spine, summoned that suffocating, terrifying intensity. Prosaically she said, 'A pleasant, interesting man.'

'Liar,' he said uncompromisingly. 'You find me a damned nuisance, just as much a nuisance as I find you. And you're every bit as aware of me as I am of you. The moment I walked into that pretty, comfortable, affluent house and saw you, tall and exquisite and profoundly, completely disturbing, I knew I wasn't going to find it easy to forget you.'

The startled breath stopped in her lungs; she sat very still, because he'd dragged her reluctant, inconvenient response to him from behind the barriers of her will and her self-discipline, and mercilessly displayed it in all its sullen power.

After swallowing to ease her dry throat, she said huskily, 'Of course I found you attractive. I'm sure most women do.'

'I'm not interested in most women.'

Gerry's heart lifted, soared, expanded. Ruthlessly she quelled the shafting pleasure, the slow, exquisitely keen delight at his admission that he wanted her with something like the basic, undiluted hunger that prowled through her veins.

But she couldn't allow it to mean anything. She said, 'I don't think now is a good time to be discussing this.'

'Look at me.' The words were growled as though compelled, as though they'd escaped the cage of his self-control.

Caught unawares, Gerry lifted her lashes. A muscle flicked in his autocratic jaw, and the beautiful sculpture of his mouth was compressed. But it was his eyes that held her captive, the pure green flames so bright her heart jumped in involuntary, automatic response. For a tense, stretched moment they rested with harsh hunger on her mouth.

And then he broke contact and said roughly, 'I agree. It's the wrong time. But it's not going to go away, Geraldine, and one day we're going to have to deal with it.'

Struggling to regain command of her emotions, she said in her most composed, most off-putting voice, 'Possibly. In the meantime, forgive me if I point out that while I tidy up here, you could employ your time better by trying to find out exactly what has gone wrong with your boat.'

He laughed and got to his feet, towering over her. 'Of course,' he said, and left the cabin.

Half an hour later she pulled the bed straight and stood up, frowning through the window. The dishes were washed and stacked away in their incredibly well-organised storage. She'd firmly resisted the urge to explore more of the kitchen. Her cabin was tidy. The bathroom had been cleaned. She didn't know what was behind the door into the other stateroom, and she wasn't looking.

So what could she do now? Apart from fret, of course.

Consciously, with considerable effort, she relaxed her facial muscles, drew in a couple of long, reviving breaths, and coaxed every tense muscle in her body to loosen.

Only when she was sure she had her face under control did she walk through the luxurious main cabin and up the short flight of stairs.

Bryn had pulled off a panel and was staring at a bewildering series of switches and wires. Although he didn't show any signs of knowing she was there, she wasn't surprised when he said shortly, 'Sometimes I think the old-fashioned ways were the best. I could probably do something about a simple engine failure.'

His tone made it obvious that it galled him to have to

admit to ignorance. In spite of her frustration, Gerry hid a smile. 'Complexity—the curse of the modern world,' she said.

Clearly he wasn't going to allude to that tense exchange over the breakfast table; it hurt that he could dismiss it so lightly and easily.

'Don't humour me,' he said abruptly, and pushed the panel back into place, screwing it on with swift, deft movements. When it was done he looked up, green eyes speculative. 'Well, Geraldine, what would you like to do? You'll get bored just sitting on the boat.'

'It depends how long we stay here,' she said coolly, not responding to the overt challenge. She looked across at a life preserver; written in red on it was the name *Starchaser*, and under it 'Auckland New Zealand', for its port of registration. 'It's a lovely boat,' she said kindly.

Bryn laughed at her. 'Thank you. Do you want to go ashore?'

The sun was too high in the sky, beating down with an intensity that warned of greater heat to come. 'Not just yet,' she said politely. 'There doesn't look to be much shelter there. I'd sooner stay on board until it cools down.'

'Then I'll show you the library.'

The books, kept in a locker in the main cabin, were an eclectic collection, ranging through biographies to solid tomes about politics and economic theory. Not a lot of fiction, she noted, and—apart from a couple of intimidating paperbacks probably left behind by guests—nothing that could be termed light. Or even medium weight.

'It doesn't look as though you read for entertainment,' she observed.

He gave her a shark's grin. 'I don't have time. I'm sorry there's nothing frothy there.'

'That,' she returned sweetly, 'sounds almost patronising, although I'm sure you didn't mean it to.'

'Sorry.'

She didn't think he was, but at least she hoped he

wouldn't make any more cracks like that. 'Readers of froth are not invariably dumb. People who like to read—real readers—usually enjoy variety in their books, and froth has its place,' she said acidly. Just to show that she wasn't impressed by his outmoded attitude, she added, 'Stereotyping is the refuge of the unreasonable.'

A swift flare of emotion in the clear green eyes startled her. 'You're the first person to ever accuse me of being unreasonable,' he said, the latent hardness in his voice very close to the surface.

'Power can isolate people.' Rather proud of the crisp mockery that ran beneath her statement, she picked up a book and pretended to read the blurb.

The written words made no sense, because Bryn was deliberately surveying her face, the enigmatic gaze scanning from her delicately pointed chin to the black lashes hiding her eyes before returning to—and lingering on—her mouth. Something untamed and fierce flamed through every cell in Gerry's body, but she bore his scrutiny without flinching. Yet that forbidden joy, that eager excitement, burst through the confines of her common sense once more.

'So can outrageous beauty,' he said.

Gerry knew that men found her desirable, and other women envied her the accident of heritage that gave her a face fitting the standards of her age. She had turned enough compliments, refused enough propositions, ignored enough gallantries, to respond with some sophistication.

Now, however, imprisoned in the glittering intensity of Bryn's gaze, her breath shortened and her heart picked up speed, and—more treasonable than either of those—heat poured through her, swift and sweet and passionate, setting her alight.

He recognised it. Harshly he said, 'I'm no more immune than any other man to the promise of a soft mouth and eyes the blue-green of a Pacific pearl, skin like sleek satin and a body that would set hormones surging through stone. If you want a quick affair, Geraldine, over as soon as we leave here, I'll be more than happy to oblige you, but don't go getting ideas that it's going to last, because it won't.'

Unable to hide her flinch, or the evidence of fading colour and flickering lashes, she kept her head high. 'No, that's not what I want, and you know it,' she said. 'I don't do one-night stands.'

CHAPTER SEVEN

BRYN'S eyes darkened and held hers for a fraught, charged moment before he said in a voice that betrayed no emotions, 'Good. It makes things much cleaner.'

He turned, and as though released from a perilous enchantment Gerry picked up a book and walked across to the stairs, hoping her erect back and straight shoulders minimised the visible effects of that excoriating exchange.

Anger swelled slow and sullen; Gerry, who hadn't lost her temper for years, had to exert her utmost will to rein it in. Because although Bryn had been unnecessarily brutal, he'd seen a danger and scotched it, and one day she'd be relieved by his cold pragmatism.

The last thing she wanted was to fall in love—or even in lust—with this man. Bryn Falconer wasn't the sort of lover a woman would get over quickly; indeed, Gerry suspected that if she let down her guard he'd take up residence in her heart, and she'd never be able to cut herself free from the turbulent alchemy of his masculinity.

And that would be ironic indeed, because by her twenty-fourth birthday she'd given up hope of finding a lasting love, one that would echo down the years.

Retreating to the shade of the canvas shelter he'd rigged over the cockpit, she sat down—back stiff, shoulders held in severe restraint, knees straight, ankles crossed—and pretended to read. The words danced dizzily, and eventually she allowed her thoughts free rein.

How many times had she thought herself in love, only to endure the death of that lovely excitement, the golden glow, with bitter resignation? At twenty-three, after breaking her engagement to a man who was perfect for her, she'd realised she was tainted by her mother's curse. After that she'd kept men at a distance. Her mother's endless search, the pain she'd caused her husbands and her children, had been a grim example, one Gerry had no intention of following.

In spite of the intensity of her infatuation for Bryn, it would die.

And she was happy with her life, apart from her dissatisfaction with her career. She loved her friends and cousins, loved their children, was loved and valued by them.

Movement from the main cabin, and the sharp click of a closing door, indicated that Bryn had gone into his stateroom; Gerry wondered why he'd slept on the sofa the previous night. Had he wanted to know when she woke so that he could tell her of their situation? A treacherous warmth invaded her heart.

He emerged almost immediately and came into the cockpit. Gerry pretended to be deep in the pages of her book, but beneath her lowered lashes her eyes followed him as he went up the stairs to the flybridge.

She could hear him moving about up there, and to block out the graphic images that invaded her mind she concentrated on reading. At first her eyes merely skipped across the pages, but eventually the written word worked its magic on her and she became lost in the book, an account of a worldwide scam that had ruined thousands of lives.

'Interesting?' Some time later Bryn's voice dragged her away from the machinations of the principal characters.

Frowning, she put the book down. 'Fascinating,' she said levelly. 'One wonders how on earth criminals can ignore the agonies of the people whose lives they're shattering.'

'One does indeed,' he said, his voice almost indifferent. 'One also gathers that you hate being interrupted when you're reading.'

Colour heated her skin. Irritated with herself for being rude enough to reveal her annoyance, and with him for being astute enough to pick it up, she said wryly, 'I do, but there's no excuse for snarling. I'm sorry.'

'I like your honesty,' he surprised her by saying, 'and you didn't snarl—you have beautiful manners which you use like a shield. When you're angry you hide behind them, and then you retreat.'

Shocked, she stared at him and felt heat flame across her cheekbones. 'Well, that's put me well and truly in my place,' she said uncertainly.

He gave her that narrow-eyed, sexy smile. 'I didn't intend to do that,' he said. 'Just a clumsy attempt to analyse what it is about you I find so intriguing. If you need anything in the next half hour or so, call out. I'm going to have a look at the engine to see if there's anything I can do.'

And he turned and went below.

Determinedly Gerry returned to her book; determinedly she followed the twists and turns of the scam, the links with drug lords, the whole filthy odyssey from genteel white-collar crime to dealing in sex and slavery and obsession. Yet as she read she was acutely aware of Bryn's movements, of the gentle swaying of the deck beneath her as he walked around below. When, some time later, he arrived in the doorway, every sense sprang into full alert.

'You'd better have something to drink,' he said. 'It's easy to dehydrate in this heat.'

Reluctantly she uncurled from the chair and followed him into the cabin. 'I'll make a pot of tea. How are we off for water?'

'There's enough if you don't spend hours in the shower.'

'No more than three minutes at a time, I promise.'

'Good.' His unsmiling look lifted the hairs on the back of her neck. 'Are you enjoying the book?'

'Not exactly *enjoying*. It's absolutely appalling, but riveting.'

He began to discuss it as though he assumed she had the intelligence to understand the complicated financial manoeuvring. So he didn't entirely think she was a flippant, flighty halfwit. And she shouldn't be comforted by this thought.

After they'd drunk the tea Bryn disappeared once more into the bowels of the boat, presumably to see whether he could find anything there that had failed. Freed from the driving necessity to appear calm, Gerry fretted about Maddie, hoping to heaven the girl was recovering, wishing that she'd seen what the problem was.

Maddie had come back from New York saying that she needed to take time to reconsider her life. Perhaps she had been trying to kick a drug habit; if only she'd said something about it, they could have helped.

It was utterly wicked that all that youth and intelligence and promise could be wiped out in the sick desire for a drug! Gerry didn't normally worry about things she couldn't change; over the years she'd learned to cultivate a practical, serene outlook. Now, however, she sat stewing until Bryn reappeared.

Her attempt to reimpose some sort of control over her features failed, for after one swift, hard glance he demanded abruptly, 'What's the matter?'

Trust him to notice. 'You mean apart from being stranded?' She relaxed her brows into their normal unconcerned arch.

'Don't worry, someone will find us soon.'

'But first they have to miss us.'

'I assume that will happen as soon as you don't arrive back in New Zealand.' He spoke patiently, as though they hadn't already had this conversation.

Gerry bit her lip. 'Of course it will. I'm sorry, I'm not helping the situation.'

Cara would begin to worry by evening. No doubt she'd ring the airline; they'd have noticed that Gerry hadn't arrived for the flight Bryn had booked for her, and as soon as they contacted the hotel on Longopai they'd realise what had happened. They'd have search parties out by tomorrow morning at the latest.

Which wouldn't be too late, if Jill, Maddie's booker, had managed to contact the ad agency...

Bryn said, 'Of course you're concerned, but you're in no danger.'

Taking refuge behind her sunglasses, Gerry gave him a collected smile. 'I know,' she said obligingly.

He'd noticed the hint of satire in her tone because his mouth tightened fractionally, but he didn't comment.

They ate lunch—a light meal of salad and fruit, and crusty bread he must have swiped from the hotel kitchen— and then Gerry tried to ease the tension that had gathered in a knot in her chest by retiring to her cabin to rest through the heat of the afternoon.

To her astonishment she slept, not waking until the sun had dipped down towards the horizon. After washing her face she combed her hair into order, pinning it back behind her ears to give her a more severe, untouchable look, then reapplied her make-up.

The main cabin was empty, but a glance up the stairs revealed Bryn standing beside the railings. Something about his stance made her skin prickle; he looked aggressive, all angles and bigness and strength.

She thought she moved as silently as he did, but his head whipped around before she'd come through the door. He surveyed her with eyes half-hidden by thick lashes.

'Good sleep?' he asked.

'Great.' She walked across to the side of the craft, stopping a few feet away from him to peer down through the crystal water. A battalion of tiny fish cast wavering shadows on the white sand beneath them. 'No signs of any rescuers?'

'No.'

Still staring at the pellucid depths, she said casually, 'So we sit and wait.'

'Basically, yes.' He sounded aloof, almost dismissive. 'I'm taking the dinghy onto the island. Want to come?'

'I'd love to. I'll just go and get my hat.'

After anchoring it to her head with a scarf around the brim she rejoined him, sunglasses hiding her eyes, her armour in place. Although he didn't look at her long, bare legs as she got into the dinghy, as she sat down on the seat she wondered uneasily whether she should have put on a pair of trousers.

Awareness was an odd thing; both of them kept it under iron control, but no doubt he could sense the response that crackled through her, just as she knew that he was acutely conscious of her, that those green eyes had noticed her feeble attempts at protection.

He moved a vicious machete well away from her feet, and began to row the inflatable across the warm blue waters of the lagoon.

'Don't tell me there's anything dangerous on the island,' she commented brightly, trying to ignore the steady, rhythmic bunching of muscles, the smooth, sure strokes, the purposeful male power that sent the small craft surging through the water.

'Not a thing. This is a foraging expedition. Note the bag to put coconuts into.'

'I thought you had an outboard motor for this dinghy?' she asked, more to keep her thoughts away from his virile energy than because she wanted to know.

'I'd rather not use it. It's unlikely, but we might need it.'

If they weren't rescued. Chilled, she nodded.

The inflatable scraped along the sand as they reached the beach. Hiding her sharp spurt of alarm with a frown, Gerry waited until the craft had come to a halt, then stepped out into water the texture of warm silk and helped Bryn haul the dinghy out of the reach of the waves. He didn't need her strength, but it gave her a highly suspect pleasure to do this with him.

Looking around, she asked, 'Do we really need coconuts?'

'Not now.' His voice was cool and judicial. 'But we

might if we don't get rescued straight away. I believe in minimising risks, so we'll drink as much coconut milk as we can bear and save the water.'

Gerry believed in minimising risks too, but at the moment all she could think of was the possibility of him falling. 'Do you know how to get up there?'

'Yes.' He gave her a brief, blinding smile. 'Don't worry, I spent a lot of time climbing coconut palms when I was a kid.'

'I didn't spend any time splinting broken limbs—as a kid or when I grew up—so you be careful,' she told him briskly.

He laughed. 'It's amazing what you can do if you have to. I could probably splint my own if it comes to that, but it won't. Don't watch.'

She should go for a walk around the island—she knew that he wouldn't do anything unless he was convinced he could. But she said, 'And miss something? Never!'

'You'd better get into the shade then.'

Retreating into the welcome coolness of the sparse undergrowth, she watched as he looped a rope around a palm bole. He certainly seemed to know what he was doing. With an economy of movement that didn't surprise her, he used the loop of rope to support him while he made his way rapidly to the tufted crown of the palm.

He was back on the ground in a very short time, nuts in a bag he'd tied around his shoulders, not even breathing heavily.

Gerry strolled across and eyed them as he dumped them in the shade. 'Now all we have to do is catch some fish and we'll really be living naturally.'

His brow lifted. 'We?'

She grinned. 'Normally I'd be squeamish,' she admitted, 'but when it comes to a matter of life and death I'm prepared to do my bit. And it's all right to kill something if you actually use it.'

'Well, that makes living on a desert island much easier,'

he said, not trying to hide the slightly caustic note in his voice. 'But we won't catch much at this time of the day. Wait until the evening. Do you want to walk around the island?'

'Yes, I'd like that.'

He smiled at her, his eyes translucent in their dark frame of lashes. 'Let's go,' he said.

The island was tiny, a dot of sand in a maze of reefs and other islets, all with their crown of palms, all too small and lacking in food and water to have permanent settlers. 'But the people from Longopai come down in the season to fish and collect coconuts,' Bryn told her. 'I've been here often. That's how I knew how to get in last night.'

Gerry looked respectfully at the reef. 'We were lucky,' she said. 'Are coconuts native to the Pacific?'

'No one knows, although most authorities believe they came from Asia. The palm's certainly colonised the tropics; in fact, if it hadn't, these islands of the Pacific could never have been settled. The Polynesians and Micronesians would have died of starvation before they reached any of the high islands where they could grow other foods. Coconuts and fish; that's what the Pacific was founded on. And that's what many live on still.'

'But it's no longer enough,' she said, thinking of the islanders who needed the money from the hats they exported to provide for their children's education.

'It never was—why do you think the Polynesians became the world's greatest explorers? But the islanders certainly want more than any atoll can provide now.'

Gerry looked around at the huge immensity of sea and sky. 'And that's unfortunate?'

He shrugged. 'No, it's merely a fact of life. The world is going to change whether I agree with it or not. Anyway, I'm glad I live now. We have great challenges, but great advantages as well.'

They walked across the thick, blinding sand, talking of the scattered island nations of the Pacific and their problems: the threat of a rising sea level, desperate attempts to balance the disruptive effects of tourism, the almost empty exchequers of many of the little countries.

It took less than twenty minutes to circle the islet. As Bryn hefted the coconuts onto his shoulder, Gerry eyed the cruiser, so big and graceful in the lagoon, and smiled ironically at its impotence.

'"How are the mighty fallen",' she quoted. 'If *Starchaser* had been a yacht we could have sailed it to Fala'isi. As it is, until it's fixed it's just a splendid piece of junk.'

'It provides us with shelter, and gas for cooking,' he said.

'True, but I'm sure you'd have been able to make some sort of shelter here on the atoll. And build a fire for cooking.'

One brow shot up. 'Yearning for the romance of a desert island?' he asked derisively. 'You wouldn't like it, Geraldine. There's no water, and you'd hate getting dirty and sweaty and hot.'

'I could do what the islanders do, and swim,' she pointed out crisply. 'You're not a romantic.'

'Not in the least.'

When he stooped to pull the little craft into the water she grabbed a loop of rope and yanked too.

'I can do it,' he said.

Strangely hurt, she stood aside until the dinghy bobbed on the surface.

'In you get,' Bryn told her. He waited until she was seated before heaving the inflatable further out into the water. Without fuss he got in himself, picked up the oars and sent the dinghy shooting through the calm, warm lagoon. 'I've lived on atolls like this and it's a lot of hard work. At least on the boat I can pump water up from the tanks manually, and we don't have to find timber for a fire every day.'

Gerry nodded. She should, she thought, looking back at the palms bending towards their reflections, be still worried sick, struggling to get back to New Zealand. But although one part of her remained anxious and alarmed, the other, seditious and unsuspecting, was more than content to be stranded in the sultry, lazy ambience of the tropics, safe with Bryn.

And that should be setting off sirens all through her, because Bryn Falconer was far from safe. Oh, he'd look after her all right, but his very competence was a threat.

In spite of that secret yearning for a soul-mate, common sense warned that loving a man as naturally dominant as Bryn would not be a peaceful experience, however seductive the lure. Her glance flashed back to Bryn's harsh-featured face and lingered for several heart-shaking moments on the subtle moulding of his mouth before returning to the shimmering, glinting, scalloped waves.

The lure, she admitted reluctantly, was *very* seductive. A forbidden hunger rose in her; she had to spurn the impulse to lean across and wipe the trickle of sweat from his temple, let her fingers tarry against the fine-grained golden skin and smooth through the tawny hair...

In other words, and let's be frank here, she told herself grimly as she swallowed to ease her parched mouth and throat, you want him.

So powerfully she could taste the need and the desire with every breath she took. This was something she couldn't control, a primeval gut-response, lust on a cellular level.

She'd fallen in love before, only to have time prove how false her emotions had been. It would happen again.

And yet—and yet there *was* a difference between the way she'd felt with other men, and the way Bryn affected her. This couldn't be curbed by will or determination; it had its own momentum, and, although she could leash any expression of it, she couldn't stifle the essential wildness of passion.

It would have been easier to deal with if he'd been Cara's lover. Oh, she'd still want him like this—no holds barred, a violent, simple matter of like calling to like—but she'd have an excellent reason for not acting on that hunger.

A gentle bump dragged her mind back from its racing thoughts to the fact that they'd reached the cruiser again. The long, corded muscles in Bryn's arms flexed as he held the dinghy in place while Gerry got shakily to her feet and climbed the steps into the cockpit.

'Catch,' he said, throwing her the rope before coming up after her, lean and big enough to block the sun.

'Give me the painter,' he commanded.

Handing the rope over, she drawled, 'Painter? Why not call it a rope, for heaven's sake?'

'Because that's not its name.'

She watched carefully as he wound the rope around the cleat. 'It doesn't look very safe,' she said, her voice sharp-edged because she hated the way he made her feel—like a snail suddenly dragged from its shell, naked and exposed. 'Shouldn't you do an interesting knot—a sheepshank, or a Turk's Head, or something Boy Scouts do?'

'Trust me,' he said on a hard note, 'it'll keep the dinghy tied on.'

'I trust you.' She turned towards the steps down to the cabin and asked over her shoulder, 'Do you want anything to drink? Tea? Coffee?'

'Something cold,' he said. 'Check out the fridge.'

His retreat into detachment was a good thing—on the boat there was little hope of avoiding each other.

Yet it stung.

Telling herself not to be a fool, Gerry extracted glasses from their cupboard—as cleverly constructed as everything else on the boat, so that even in the worst seas nothing would break—and poured lime juice over ice before carrying them up to the cockpit. Bryn was staring at the horizon, watchful green eyes unreadable beneath the dark brows.

'Here,' she said, offering the glass.

He turned abruptly and took it, careful not to let his fingers touch hers, and drank it down. 'Thanks,' he said, handing over the glass without looking at her.

Rebuffed, Gerry went back to the kitchen and drank her juice there.

Let someone find them soon, she prayed, before she did something stupid like letting Bryn see just how much she wanted him.

CHAPTER EIGHT

To HER relief they spent the rest of the day at a polite distance. While Bryn poked about the internal regions of the boat, Gerry wondered about washing her clothes, finally deciding against it. She didn't know how much water the tanks held, and she had enough clean underwear for three days. They certainly wouldn't take long to dry in the minuscule bathroom.

The afternoon sun poured relentlessly in through the cabin windows. Although she opened them, in the hope of fresh air, eventually the heat drove her into the cockpit where, still hot under the awning, she read, keeping her attention pinned very firmly to the printed page.

Towards sunset Bryn got out fishing lines from lockers in the cockpit.

Looking up, Gerry asked, 'Can I help?'

'No, I'll take the dinghy out into the centre of the lagoon.'

He didn't ask her to go with him, and she didn't offer. In the rapidly fading light Gerry kept her eyes on the western sky, watching the sun silkscreen it into a glory of gold and red and orange, until with a suddenness that startled her the great smoky ball hurtled beneath the horizon. As the last sliver disappeared a ray of green light—the colour of Bryn's eyes—stabbed the air, a vivid, astonishing flash that lasted only a second before dusk swept across the huge immensity of sky, obliterating all colour, cloaking everything in heated velvet darkness.

Gerry stared into the dense nothingness until her eyes adjusted to the lack of light. A few hundred metres away she could see the outline of the dinghy with Bryn in it—

patient, predatory, still—and was amazed by her sudden atavistic fear at the contrast between that stillness and his usual vital energy. A moment later she detected a swift movement, and shortly afterwards the dinghy headed back towards the cruiser.

Determined not to spend the rest of the evening in the same silence as the afternoon, Gerry met him with a smile. 'And what, oh mighty hunter, did you catch?'

He laughed shortly. 'A careless fish.'

She'd expected a whole fish, but he'd already filleted and scaled it. 'Will it be all right fried?' she asked.

'Unless you have more exotic ways of dealing with it.'

'I'm your basic cook—and that's probably overstating the case—so I'll stick to the tried and true,' she said, adding with a hint of mischief, 'Of course, you could cook it.'

His eyes gleamed in the starlight. 'I think the traditional division of duties is that I catch and kill, you cook.'

'You Tarzan, me Jane,' she said, laughing. 'That went out with the fifties.'

'Not entirely.'

'In any civilised country,' she retorted, heading down the companionway and thence into the kitchen. Perhaps she should try to think of it as the galley. You're getting used to this lazy life out of life, she warned herself severely. Be careful, Gerry.

'We're not in a civilised country here,' he said, following her.

'So it's lucky that I'm quite happy to cook,' she parried, aware of something else running through the conversation, a hidden current of provocation, of advance and retreat, of unspoken challenge.

Too dangerous.

She made the mistake of looking up at him. He was smiling, a mirthless, fierce smile that didn't soften his face at all.

Gerry's heart gave a wild thump; without volition she took a step backwards, and although she held her head high and kept her gaze steady she knew he'd seen and noted that moment of weakness.

'*Can* you cook it?' he asked, lounging against the bar that separated the galley from the main cabin.

She took the fish and slid it onto a plate and into the fridge. 'I'll manage,' she said evenly.

'Then I'll leave you to get on with it.'

Gerry's breath came soundlessly through her lips as he straightened up and walked towards his cabin. 'Damned arrogant man,' she muttered as she pulled out a tin of coconut cream. She didn't like arrogance; both the men she'd thought she'd loved had been kind and pleasant and intelligent and tolerant.

Nothing like Bryn Falconer.

Banishing him from her mind, she wondered whether perhaps she should use the coconut he'd got that day. Except that she didn't know how you turned the milk in it into the cream you bought in tins—suitable for delicious oriental-style sauces that were especially suitable for fish.

'Give me modern conveniences every time,' she muttered as she found the tin opener in its special slot in a drawer.

Bryn emerged as she was lowering the floured fish fillets into the big frying pan. Through the delicate sizzle she heard him close the door; she didn't look over her shoulder, but as he went past she thought she smelt his clean, just-washed fragrance.

'Would you like some wine?' he asked.

Then she did look up, and once more her heart lurched. He'd changed into a short-sleeved shirt and fine cotton trousers. Lean-hipped, long-legged, he moved with a smooth grace that pulled at her senses.

'Yes, thank you,' she said simply. Keep it light, her common sense warned her. Pretend that this is just another man, just another occasion.

He reached into what she'd assumed to be another cupboard. It was a bar fridge, from which he pulled out a bottle of wine. Once more everything was stored so carefully that it was safe whatever the height of the waves.

'All mod cons on this boat,' she teased as he removed the cork in one deft movement and poured the subtly coloured, gold-green vintage into two elegant glasses. 'It's more luxurious than my house.'

He picked up a glass, set it down close to her. 'Even you,' he said calmly, 'must know that boats are referred to as women, so she's she, not it.'

'All these funny traditions! Why?'

'Perhaps because they're inherently beautiful,' he said, his voice a blend of whisky and cream, of honey and dark, potent magic. 'And dangerous. And therefore profoundly attractive to men.'

Gerry turned the fillets of fish with great care before she could trust herself to answer. Picking up the glass of wine, she lifted it to her lips and took a small, desperate sip. Then she set it down and allowed herself a smile, although it felt cold and stiff on her lips. 'An interesting theory,' she said lightly, dismissively, 'but I think it's just part of the desire to confuse the uninitiated—which is why the kitchen is a galley and a rope is a painter. It's jargon, and it connects people with the same interests so that they can feel part of a common brotherhood, shutting others out.'

'Feeling lost and alone, Geraldine?'

Ashamed at the snap in her words, she shrugged. 'I suppose I am.'

'Don't you trust me to look after you?' A steely thread of mockery ran beneath the words.

She bit her lip. 'Of course I do,' she said, keeping her voice steady.

'Then it must be the situation back in Auckland.'

Shocked by the strength of her temptation to tell him all about it, she poked gingerly at the fish fillets. Bryn was a hard man, and sometimes she could kick him, but he would know how to deal with almost anything that came his way. However, the problem wasn't hers to tell. Maddie had a future—Gerry refused to believe otherwise—and the fewer people who knew about her addiction the better.

Even though Cara would probably tell Bryn once they got back to Auckland.

No, not if she was asked not to. Cara was young, and she could be foolish, but she was trustworthy.

'Partly,' Gerry said coolly, 'but there's nothing I can do about that so I'm trying not to worry. Besides, Honor McKenzie, my partner, is probably back by now and dealing with it.'

'A very pragmatic attitude.'

'My father was big on being sensible.'

'If I had a daughter who looked like you I'd do my best to bring her up to be sensible,' Bryn agreed lazily.

Yet James Dacre had worked himself into the grave saving a business that had been run into the ground by a greedy manager, who'd then decamped into the unknown with everything James had spent his lifetime building. He hadn't been sensible, but he'd been honourable.

Tight-lipped, Gerry said, 'He was a man who believed in responsibility.'

'I know.'

Gerry pulled the frying pan from the gas ring and lifted each perfect, golden piece onto a plate, warm from the oven. Picking up the plates and heading towards the table, which she'd set while Bryn was showering, she said, 'He paid back every last dollar the firm owed before he died.'

He carried a bowl of pasta salad across to the table. 'Leaving you with nothing.'

If he'd sounded curious, or even sympathetic, she'd have been short with him, but his voice revealed nothing more than a cool impersonality. 'That wasn't important,' she said crisply as she set the plates down. 'I can make my own way. But it'll be a cold day in hell before I forgive the man who sent my father to an early grave. I just wish I knew where he is now.'

Bryn's enigmatic glance lingered on her angry face. 'Do you have a taste for vengeance?'

She sat down. After a moment she said flatly, 'No. I'd like to, because nothing would give me greater pleasure than to see the man who killed my father in exactly the same situation—sick, tired, so exhausted that in the end nothing mattered any more. Dad used to say that eventually you reap what you sow. He didn't, but it gives me some comfort to believe that of the man who drove him to his death.'

'Eat up,' Bryn said, his voice unexpectedly gentle.

Obeying, Gerry was eventually able to taste the food she'd prepared. She finished her glass of wine a little more quickly than was wise, so refused another, and was oddly pleased when Bryn only drank one too.

Over the meal they spoke of impersonal things; Bryn's attitude reminded her of the day they'd met. He'd been gentle then too, holding the baby with strength and security and comfort. He'd be a good father.

What would he be like as a husband?

'That's an odd smile,' he said idly.

'I was hoping that the baby is all right.'

'Unfortunately that's all you can do—hope.' He'd helped her clean up and wash the dishes, then banished her while he made coffee. Now he came from behind the bar and handed her a cup and saucer. 'What made you think of her?'

'I don't know.' She put the coffee down on the table in front of her and frowned. 'Bryn, why on earth should everything die on the boat? Surely the communications and the engine don't work off the same systems?'

'No.'

He sat down beside her, alarming her. She could cope when he was opposite her—she was fine with the table between them, or a metre or so of space. But the sofa seemed very small suddenly, and his closeness stifled every ounce of common sense. Swallowing unobtrusively, she sat up straighter, trying to keep her eyes on the steam that swirled up from her coffee.

'Occasionally kids from Longopai get into the *Starchaser*,' he said. 'I can't say it was definitely them, but someone removed most of the diesel; that same someone left the communications system on so that the batteries are completely drained.'

'I'm surprised you're not furious,' she said, ironing out the husky note in her tone into a somewhat clipped curtness.

His crystalline gaze flicked across her face and his smile sizzled right through her. It was, she thought, as elemental as a force of nature. Did he know its effect on susceptible women?

Almost certainly. He was too intelligent not to.

'I can remember what I was like at ten,' he said, wry laughter in his words. 'All devilry and flash, keen to see how things worked; I'd have examined *Starchaser* from bow to stern, from propeller to aerial, and I'd probably have drained the battery as well.'

'And stolen the diesel?' she asked.

He shrugged. 'You know as well as I do that to Polynesians what belongs to a brother belongs to you, and on Longopai I'm everyone's brother. Someone needed it. They'll replace it. If we hadn't had to get away so quickly I'd have been told there wasn't enough fuel to get me to Fala'isi.' Unsmiling, he added, 'In fact, they're probably out looking for us now.'

God, Gerry thought, drinking her coffee too fast, I hope they find us first thing tomorrow.

He asked suddenly, 'What have you done to your finger?'

'Cut it while I was chopping the onions. It's nothing.'

He held out an imperative hand. 'Let me see.'

While she hesitated he took her hand and turned it over, examining the small cut with frowning eyes. 'It looks deep.'

'It's fine,' she said quickly, tugging away.

To no avail. Bryn ran the tip of a finger across the cut and then, without pausing, down and across her palm. The touch that had been comforting changed in a few short centimetres to wildly sensuous.

He must have heard the sharp, indrawn breath she couldn't control, but he lifted her hand to his mouth and kissed the small cut, and the palm of her hand before saying harshly, 'I'll get some antiseptic. Cuts can become badly infected in the tropics.'

Numbly, fingers curling, she watched him head towards a drawer. The place he'd kissed burned, echoing the fire that swept through her blood.

He took a tube from the drawer and tossed it to her with the curt command, 'Rub it well in, and put it on several times a day.'

Eagerly Gerry bent her head and unscrewed the cap, and smoothed the pale ointment onto her finger.

It stung a little, but she ignored the pain to babble into the tense silence, 'It's nice that you're still so close to the islanders you grew up with. I have a vast number of cousins, but I always wanted real brothers and sisters.'

'Don't you have two brothers?'

'Half-brothers,' she said. 'From different fathers—one in America, one in France. I've met them occasionally, and we have nothing in common. My father did his best to turn me into a lady, but I'd have liked brothers to be mischievous with.'

'You have enough of an advantage now,' he said harshly.

Startled, she looked up, into eyes as unfathomable as the wide ocean. Her breath came quickly. 'I don't know what you mean,' she said stupidly.

'I think you do,' he said, irony underscoring each word. 'You know how you affect men. The first time I saw you I thought you were a dark-eyed witch—half-devil, half-angel, all woman—with a smile that promised the delights of paradise. And then I realised that your eyes are a fascinating, smoky mixture of blue's innocence and green's provocation, and I was lost...'

Spellbound by the gathering passion that roughened his voice, she let him pull her up and into his arms. She had known he was strong—now she felt that strength, the virile force and power, and her immediate, ardent response sang through her like a love song as Bryn's mouth found her lashes and kissed them down, traced the high sweep of each cheekbone, the square chin. Bryn's scent—fresh, fiercely male—filled her nostrils, and his mouth on her skin was heaven, gentle and powerful and agonising. Dazed, she heard her own wordless murmur as she lifted her face in supplication.

Yet he didn't take the gift so freely offered. Instead his lips found the pulse-point beneath her ears, the soft, vulnerable throbbing in her throat, and each time he touched her fire licked through her veins.

It stunned her with its heat, with its intensity. The only point of contact was his mouth, a slow, potent pledge of rapture against her waiting, welcoming skin. It was insulting, this deliberate display of control when Gerry was rapidly losing the ragged threads of hers. Harried by desperation, she wanted to feel his hands on her—had been wanting that ever since she'd met him, even though she'd believed he was Cara's lover.

For a moment she held back, remembering that she should be worrying about Maddie, and then he kissed the corner of her mouth, tormenting her with a promise of passion, a compulsion of desire such as she'd never experienced before.

She didn't hear his laugh; she felt it, a quick brush of air against her skin, a recognition that he knew what he was doing to her. Splintered by a sudden, dangerous fury, she forced her heavy lids upwards and clenched her hands on his arms.

'Wait,' she commanded.

'Why?' he asked, narrowed eyes green diamonds set in thick black lashes. A smile curled the ruthless mouth.

Swift shock ran the length of Gerry's spine, but she tried again. 'Stop teasing me,' she said, hearing the helpless, hopeless note of need in her voice.

'How am I teasing you?'

Still angry, she reached up and kissed him boldly on his taunting, beautiful mouth.

She wanted to pull back immediately, to show him that she wasn't completely mesmerised, but it was too late. When her lips met his he laughed again and crushed her to him, strong hands moulding her against his body, his mouth ravishing every thought from her brain.

It was like being taken over, she thought just before she succumbed to the hunger that had been building in her ever since she'd looked over a baby's downy head and met his eyes.

He no longer kept up the farce of gentleness, of tenderness. He kissed her with the driving determination of a man who had finally slipped the leash of his will-power and allowed his desire free rein. Gerry's curbed hunger exploded, overwhelming every warning, every ounce of common sense her father had tried to drum into her.

With molten urgency she returned Bryn's kiss. Her pulses galloped as he lifted her and sat down on the sofa with her in his arms, and without taking his mouth from hers pulled her across his knees and slid his hand beneath the wrap-around front of her blouse, fingers cupping her breast.

Sensation rocketed through her. Her mouth opened and he took swift advantage, thrusting deep in a blatant simulation of the embrace both of them knew was coming. Gerry twisted under the remorseless lash of desire; every sense was overloaded. Bryn's experienced caress was transformed into an unbearably stimulating friction that smashed through the remaining fragile barriers of her will.

His taste was pure male, exotic, stimulating, his arms a

welcome, longed-for prison, the surface texture of his chest exquisitely erotic to the tips of her fingers as she unsteadily pulled the buttons of his shirt free and ran her hand across the heated skin below.

Gerry felt his shudder like a benediction.

'Yes, you like that,' he said, lifting his head so that the words touched her lips, to be drunk in without too much attention to meaning. 'You like the power your beauty gives you, the way men respond to the primitive allure beneath that sophisticated, glossy outer appearance. I'm just like all the rest, Geraldine—I want you. But what do you want? Because if this keeps on for much longer I'm not going to be able to stop.'

She lifted weighted eyelids, met the blazing green of his eyes with a slow smile. 'You,' she said, and because her voice shook, she tried again. 'I want you.'

Something perilously close to satisfaction flared in his eyes. 'Good.'

Her lashes drifted down, but instead of kissing her eager mouth he shocked her by pushing back the lapel of her shirt and kissing the soft skin his hand so possessively caressed.

Fire seared away everything but the hunger that shattered her last vestige of composure. Her legs straightened, and she stiffened, blind to everything but the savage need to take and be taken.

When his mouth closed around the tip of her breast a hoarse, low sound was torn from her throat, to be lost in the conflagration of her senses. He began to suckle and she gasped again, splaying her hands over his chest, blindly seeking satisfaction. The delicate friction of his body hair against her hot skin shivered from her fingers to the pit of her stomach.

On impulse she turned her head and sought the small male nipple and copied his actions, an intimacy she'd never offered before, never known. Under her cheek his chest

wall lifted, and she heard the beat of his heart, heavy, demanding.

'Geraldine,' he muttered, his voice reverberating through
her.

And when he got to his feet and carried her into her cabin
she made no protest.

Stranded in the dazzling, shape-shifting haze he'd conjured around her, she lay back against the pillows and
watched with unsated eyes while he tore off his shirt and
the trousers she'd admired earlier. No hesitation spoiled the
moment, no fear—nothing but a glowing anticipation that
wrapped her in silken fur, clawed at her with primal, eager
hunger.

With the light from the main cabin reflecting lovingly on
Bryn's golden skin, he came down beside her and said with
an odd thickness in his voice, 'I seem to have thought of
nothing but this since I first saw you—lovely, elusive
Geraldine, lying in my bed, waiting for me...'

Deft hands slipped her shirt from her, smoothed her
shorts down. She shivered at the skill with which he un-
dressed her, shivered again—and for a different reason—
when the long fingers stroked down her legs, lingering
across the smooth skin on the inside of her thighs before
moving to her calves.

'Fine-boned and elegant,' he said, and found her ankles
and her feet.

She had to clear her throat to say, 'I've never thought of
my calves and feet as erotic zones.'

'Haven't you?' He sounded amused, and bent and kissed
the high arch. As her foot curled in involuntary reaction he
said in a deeper voice, 'Every part of a responsive woman
is an erotic zone. If you don't know that it's high time you
learned.'

She learned. Where Bryn wanted to go was where she
wanted to be, and he wreaked such dark havoc with his
mouth and his enormously skilled, knowledgeable hands
that in a few minutes he'd proved his statement and she

was begging for mercy, her body craving the consummation only he could give her.

'Not yet,' he said huskily. 'Not yet, little witch.'

In self-defence she tried to turn the tables by caressing him, but perhaps she lacked the experience, for when she had completely unravelled he was still master of himself—and of her body's responses.

By then, wild-eyed and panting, she didn't care.

'Now,' she gasped, almost sobbing as she finally pulled at his broad shoulders.

Later she would remember that they were slick with sweat, and that his eyes were hooded slivers of glittering emerald, so focused that she thought they burned wherever they rested. But at that moment she was completely at the mercy of her body's need for completion, torn by this unfamiliar passion.

In answer he came over her and entered her violent, supplicating body in one strong thrust.

Gerry gasped. He froze, the big, lithe body held in stasis. 'You should have warned me that it's been a long time for you,' he said, his voice raw with barely maintained control.

He was going to leave her. He thought he'd hurt her so he was going to abandon her to this savage, unfulfilled need.

'It's all right—it doesn't matter,' she said, her voice thready in the quiet cabin.

He said something so crude she flinched. 'It matters,' he growled. Beneath her importuning hands she felt the swift coil and bunching of muscles as he prepared to get up.

She looked up into a face stripped of everything but anger. Driven by a merciless compulsion, she fastened her arms across his broad back and offered herself to him, arching beneath him, flexing muscles she hadn't known she had, moving slowly, sensuously against him.

'No!' he commanded.

Gerry thought she'd lost, but within seconds she saw her triumph in his eyes as the anger prowling in the metallic opacity was joined by a consuming hunger, basic, white-hot.

Her heart jerked within her chest. Bryn withdrew, but only to bury himself again to the hilt in her, and as she enclosed him in her heated flesh, tightening her arms around his back to pull him down against her, he said, 'This is what you want, isn't it?'

She couldn't answer, and he demanded, 'Gerry?'

'Yes, damn you!' she shouted, twisting her hips against him.

He curled his fingers in her hair, holding her face back so that he could see it. This was not satisfaction—that was far too weak a term to use. On his face was exultation, pure and simple, and she couldn't deny him it because it was her victory too.

With deliberation, with authority and steady male power, he began to move in her. Holding his gaze, she locked her feet around his calves and returned movement for movement, passion for passion, until the knot of pleasure inside her began to unravel, sending her soaring, hurtling over some distant edge and into a world where nothing existed but she and Bryn, and the boat moving slightly, peacefully beneath them in the embrace of the Pacific.

A starburst of rapture tore a cry from her and she imploded into ecstasy, stiffening into rigidity, and then, when the exquisite savagery began to fade, responding anew to Bryn's desire.

And soon, even as the fresh nova ripped through her, she saw his head go back and a fierce, mirthless grin pull his lips into a line as he too found that place where nothing else mattered.

Like that, they lay until their breaths slowed and their hearts eased and sleep claimed them.

Much later, after she'd slept in his arms and they'd woken and made love again—love that had started slow and lazy, without the edge of unsated desire, and then exploded into

incandescent passion, desperate and all-consuming—Gerry
yawned, a satisfying gape that almost cracked her face in
two, and eased herself free.

'Where are you going?' he asked, his voice husky.

'Bathroom,' she muttered.

'Head,' he said lazily. 'On a boat it's called the head.'

He was laughing at her, and she laughed too, and kissed
the curved line of his mouth and said, 'Whatever, I need
to shower. I'm sticky.' A thought struck her. 'Have we
enough water and power for frivolous showers?'

'Plenty, if we shower together.'

'It's too small,' she protested.

'We'll fit.'

They did—just. Bryn laughed at her shocked face.

'It's not decent,' she said demurely, 'and it's too hot.'

'The water will cool us down.'

Green eyes gleamed as he soaped her, became heavy-
lidded and purposeful when she insisted on doing the same
for him.

'You're as sleek as a panther,' she said from behind him,
sliding wet hands across his back.

'Panthers have fur.'

Gerry linked her hands across his chest and pressed her
cheek against his shoulderblade. 'Mmm,' she said slowly,
'I'd like that.'

Beneath her palms she felt his chest lift as he laughed.

The water sputtered and she let him go so that he could
turn around and rinse the soap off. A lean hand turned the
shower off, then he looped an arm around her and kissed
her, hard and fast, before picking her up. As he edged by
the rack he grabbed a towel and tossed it onto the bed, and
her in the middle of it, and came down and made love to
her with a ferocity that blew her mind.

Gerry woke to a voice, a low murmur that teased the
edge of her hearing. Almost as soon as her tired brain registered what was happening, the sound died into silence,
and before she had a chance to get up Bryn came in through

the door. Opening her eyes, she saw that it was dawn, a still, soft light that held the promise of delight.

But not as much as Bryn's slow, possessive survey.

'Who were you talking to?' she asked, smothering a yawn with the back of her hand.

His brows rose. 'Talking? No—oh, I did express my opinion of his thieving habits to a gull that tried to snatch the bait from my line.'

'Did you catch any fish?'

'I lost the urge,' he said gravely, sitting down on the bed.

Colour leaped again through her skin. He was wearing a terrible old pair of shorts, but he at least had some clothes on whereas she had nothing.

'You blush from your heart upwards,' he said, a dark finger tracing the uppermost curves of her breasts.

Drugged with satiation, she said languidly, 'I suppose everyone does.'

'I don't blush,' he said.

'Neither do I, normally.'

'And we established very effectively last night that this isn't normal behaviour for you,' he said without much expression.

'I wasn't a virgin,' she said, 'but I don't make a habit of—' her skin warmed again when he moved a curl back from her cheek and tucked it behind her ear '—of sleeping with men I barely know.'

'At first I thought you were—a virgin, I mean.'

'It had been a long time.'

'We didn't get much sleep,' he said absently. 'You must be tired.'

Raising her head, she bit his shoulder, quite hard, then licked the salty skin. She could hear the sudden harshness of his breathing.

'I'm hungry,' she said demurely.

He laughed deep in his throat and turned her towards him, his eyes fierce and primal. 'So am I,' he said, taking her with him as he slid down onto the tumbled sheets. 'Let's see what we can do about it, shall we?'

Later—an hour or so later—Gerry yawned prodigiously and muttered, 'You're insatiable.' Each word slurred off her tongue.

Bryn kissed her. 'Apparently,' he said lazily.

Something in his tone alerted her, but her eyes were heavy and she could feel waves of exhaustion creeping up from her toes, dragging her further and further into unconsciousness. Although she tried for clearer pronunciation, her words ran together again. 'What bothers me is that I seem to be too...'

He said something, but she couldn't fathom it out, didn't even want to. The rumble of his voice was the last sound she heard before sleep, voracious and draining, claimed her.

CHAPTER NINE

GERRY woke to find the sun high in the sky. Dry-mouthed, filmed with sweat, she stretched, aware of the change in Bryn's breathing as he too woke. Her body ached pleasantly, and when she moved she felt a slight tenderness between her legs.

And although she'd spent the night in his arms, now, more than ever, she craved the protection of her cosmetics.

She croaked, 'I need another shower and a large glass of water. I think I'm dehydrated.'

He laughed. 'I've got a better idea.'

Naked and entirely confident, he got to his feet and stooped over her, eyes glittering, dark face intent. Gerry's heart leapt in her breast, but he picked her up and carried her through the cabin and out into the cockpit. She smiled as she realised what he planned to do. No man had ever carried her around before, no man had ever made her so sure of herself, so positive in her sexuality.

He jumped with her still in his arms. Supple and languid from the night, Gerry welcomed the cool embrace of the sea, an embrace that soon turned warm. They sank down through the water; opening her eyes, Gerry squinted at the sun-dazzle above, and the harsh lines of Bryn's face, arrogant, tough, exultant.

As his legs propelled them towards the surface she wondered how such a man could be as tender as he was fiery, both gentle and ruthless, a dominant male who refused to take his own satisfaction until his lover had reached the peak of her ecstasy. Her previous lover had been considerate, but nothing she'd experienced came anywhere near the transcendent sensuality of Bryn's lovemaking.

Chilled, she realised that he'd set a benchmark; when this idyll was over she might never find another man who could love her as he had. Was this aching sense of loneliness and incompletion the goad that had spurred her mother on her futile search?

In an explosion of crystals they burst through the surface into the kiss of the sun, and she broke away from him, striking out for the island.

It was further than she thought. Although a good swimmer, she was tired when she got there. Not so Bryn, who kept pace easily with her. As they walked through the shallows and side by side across the white unsullied sand, Gerry thought they were like Adam and Eve, and wished futilely that they didn't have to return to their responsibilities.

He waited until they'd reached the shelter of the palms before asking, 'Do you want to eat breakfast here?'

It would be a perfect way to end this time out of time. Today someone would come looking for them and they would go their separate ways. Oh, in spite of his specific denial, they might resume their affair in Auckland, but it would never again be like this. The mundane world had a habit of tarnishing romance.

And that belief too she'd probably inherited from her mother.

Gerry pushed her hair back from her face. 'I'd love to.'

'OK, stay here in the shade. I'll swim back to the boat and load up the dinghy.'

'What if you get a cramp?' Stupid, she thought despairingly. Oh, that was stupid. Why fuss over a man so obviously able to look after himself?

'I know how to deal with it,' he told her calmly, his eyes transparent as the water, cool and limpid and unreadable. 'And if a shark comes by I'd be much happier knowing you weren't in the water with me.'

She cast a startled glance around. 'Are there sharks here?'

'It's not likely.' He set off towards the water.

Gerry watched while his strong tanned arms clove the water, only relaxing when he hauled himself up into the cruiser and waved.

Swimming had cleared some of the sensuous miasma from her brain, but she needed to think about the fact that during the night she had surrendered much more than her body to Bryn—she had handed over a part of her heart.

It terrified her.

Biting her lip, she stared down at the strappy leaves of a small plant, tough and dry on this waterless island, a far cry from the usually lush tropical growth. Idly she began to plait the leaves together.

Long ago she'd become reconciled to the fact that she was like her mother. Oh, she fell in love—no problem there. Only then, inevitably, she fell out of love. Sooner or later her dreaded boredom crept in, draining each relationship of joy and interest.

This time it might be different; Bryn was nothing like the other men she'd loved.

'No,' she muttered. She'd gone through this exercise before—tried to convince her sensible inner self that what she felt was real and true, an emotion enduring enough to transcend time and familiarity.

A stray breeze creaked through the fronds of the coconut palms above. Frowning, she rubbed her eyes. Last night Bryn had kissed her lashes down; her breath came quickly as she recalled things he'd said, the raw, rough sound of his voice, the sinfully skilled hands...

Impossible to believe that she'd ever grow tired of him!

But that was just sex, and Bryn was a magnificent lover. Gerry might not be experienced—her second love affair, six years ago, had been her only other physical relationship—but she recognised experience and, she thought grimly, a great natural talent. Bryn knew women.

Surely she'd never be able to look at him without responding to his heart-jolting impact!

And it wasn't just sex. He was sharp and tough and intelligent, he made her laugh, he refused to let her get away with using her charm instead of logic—oh, he fascinated her.

Would that last? Perhaps. She knew couples who still preferred each other's company after years of marriage.

Emotionally, however, he was uncharted territory.

Appropriate, she thought, her fingers stilling as she looked around the tiny islet. Bryn was a desert island—she understood nothing of his emotions, his feelings. And so, she thought painfully, was she. She had never known the particular power of transformation that accompanied such unselfconscious selflessness.

Even if he was the one man who could fix her wayward emotions—he'd shown no signs of loving her. Oh, he'd enjoyed taking her, and he'd met and matched her gasping, frenzied response with his own dynamic male power—but he didn't know her, so how could he love her? And in spite of the dark sexual enchantment that bedazzled them both, she suspected that he didn't like her much.

Even if he hadn't stated that it wouldn't last, they had no future.

It hurt even to think it, but Gerry fought back an icy pang of desolation to face facts squarely. And once she'd forced herself to accept them, her way was clear.

She'd enjoy this passionate interlude and then she'd end it before it had a chance to fizzle into damp embers. That way they'd both keep their dignity.

Some unregenerate part of her wondered just how Bryn would take a dignified dismissal. That bone-deep assurance indicated a man unused to rejection. Perhaps he'd pursue her, she thought with a flash of heat.

Why should he? cold logic demanded mockingly. He'd understand. What they shared was sex, and Bryn could get that from almost any woman he wanted. Why should he care if she turned him down? Beyond a momentary blow to his ego it wouldn't mean a thing.

She gazed at the pattern she'd made with the long leaves

of the plant. An ironic smile hurt her mouth. Somehow she'd managed to weave them together into a lopsided heart. Swiftly, deftly, she separated them, straightened out a couple she'd twisted, and turned back to the beach.

Bryn was almost there, the sun gilding his skin as he rowed the dinghy in. Until then Gerry hadn't bothered about her nakedness, but now she felt conspicuous and stupidly shy.

'Stay in the shade,' he called as the dinghy grounded on the glaring sand. 'I'll bring the stuff up.'

She waited in the shade, absently scratching a runnel of salt on her forearm. Naked, moving easily and lithely around the small craft, Bryn's sheer male energy blazed forth with compelling forcefulness. Incredibly, desire clutched her stomach, ran like electricity through her nerves, sparked synapses through her entire body. All that strength, she thought dizzily, all that power, and for a short time—for a few racing hours—it had been hers.

A hamper under one arm, something that turned out to be a rolled up rug under the other, he strode across the sand like a god worshipped by the sun, muscles moving with unstudied litheness beneath the mantle of golden skin.

Erotic need turned into a ripple, a current, a torrent of hunger. Gerry drew in a deep, ragged breath. Damn it, she'd never been at the mercy of her urges, and she wasn't going to start now!

She'd thought she'd succeeded in controlling her reaction, but Bryn took one look at her set face and asked, 'What's the matter?'

'Nothing.'

Although he wasn't satisfied, he didn't pursue it. Handing her the rug, he said, 'Spread this out, will you?'

She found a spot between bushes, shaded and secluded, yet with enough breeze for comfort. Bryn set the hamper down and helped her with the rug, then tossed her a length of cotton coloured in startling greens and blues and an intense muted colour halfway between them both.

'I thought you might want a pareu,' he said drily as he wound another length, in tans and ochres and blacks, around his lean hips.

With shaking fingers Gerry wrapped herself in the cotton, tucking two corners in just above her breasts to make a strapless sundress. Keeping her face turned away from him, she knelt on the rug to examine the contents of the hamper.

'My grandfather used to say,' Bryn told her as she took the lid off the hamper, 'that only a fool allowed himself to be manoeuvred into an untenable situation. If someone finds us while we're eating breakfast, I'd rather be clothed.'

'Me too,' she said fervently, looking up.

He smiled, and it was like being hit in the heart with a cannonball of devilish, sexually-charged charm. No man, she thought, setting out delicious slices of pawpaw and melon, should be able to do that. It gave him a totally unfair advantage.

'Here,' he said, offering her a tube of sunscreen. 'I didn't bring your make-up, but this will give you some protection.'

'Thank you,' she said stiltedly, wishing that he wasn't so astute. Of all her acquaintanceship only Bryn seemed to have realised that cosmetics were the shield she donned against a prying world.

Hastily she spread the lotion onto her face and arms and legs, on the soft swell of her breast above the cotton pareu, and as far down her back as she could reach.

When she'd finished, he said, 'Turn around, I'll do the rest.'

Even slick with sunscreen, the power and strength of his hands set her nerve-ends oscillating, sending tiny shocks through her body.

'You have such an elegant back,' he said evenly. 'But then, you're elegant all over, from the way you walk, the way you hold your head on that slim, poised neck, to the graceful, spare lines of your face and throat and body, the narrow wrists and fragile ankles—and that air of fine, steely strength and courage.' His hands swept up across her shoulders and fastened loosely around her throat, his fingertips resting against the turbulent pulse at its base. 'A true thoroughbred,' he said, the latent harshness in his voice almost reaching the surface.

She had to swallow, and his fingers would have felt her tense muscles. 'A fortunate genetic heritage,' she said. 'Like yours.'

He laughed and withdrew his hands. 'From a beach bum and a spoilt, frail little rich girl?' he asked sardonically.

Reaching for the tube, she said, 'Turn around and I'll put sunscreen on you.' She was playing with fire, but she didn't care. Some note in his voice had made her wince, and she needed to try and make things better for him.

For a moment she thought he'd refuse, but almost immediately he presented his back to her, the smooth golden skin taut and warm over the muscles beneath—the shape of a man, she thought fancifully, cupping her palm to receive the sunscreen. Her hands tingled as she spread the liquid.

'Even if your father wasn't the most responsible man in the world,' she said, 'he had the guts to actually do what many men only dream of. And so did your mother. Has it ever occurred to you that your father knew you'd be well looked after when he left Longopai? Or that he probably intended to come back?'

'An optimist as well,' he jeered. 'No, it hasn't.'

Aware that she'd trespassed onto forbidden ground, she massaged the lotion into his skin. 'Then at least you should take credit for overcoming your heredity.'

His shoulders lifted as he laughed, deep and low and humourless. 'Perhaps I should thank heaven that I had such a brilliant example of what not to do, how not to be. At least I accept responsibility for my actions. And for my mistakes. Have you finished there?'

'Yes.' She recapped the tube and gave it to him to pack, then poured them both coffee.

With little further conversation they ate breakfast, a feast of fruit, plus rolls he'd taken from the freezer and heated in the oven. Passionfruit jelly oozed across the moist white bread, tangy and sweet, and the coffee he'd carried in a Thermos scented the salt-laden air.

'A truly magnificent repast,' Gerry sighed, sucking a spot of jelly from the tip of one finger. Looking up, she caught Bryn's green gaze on her mouth, and grinned. 'And don't tell me your grandfather used to insist on table napkins at all times. So did my father, but I still lick the occasional finger.'

'You shouldn't be allowed to,' he said.

Eyes widening, she stared at him.

'It's all right,' he said roughly. 'I do have some self-control. We'd better get back on board.'

It was an excuse to move, and she leapt to her feet with alacrity. Although desire pulsed through her with swift, merciless power, making love again would stretch already over-strung muscles and tissues.

Working swiftly, they repacked the hamper and folded the rug. Swiftly they walked across the scorching sand, and swiftly made their way across the peacock water to the sleek white cruiser.

Once she was aboard, Bryn handed up the hamper. 'Leave it there, I'll carry it below,' he said. 'Here, take the painter and cleat it.'

Gerry took the rope—the painter, she corrected herself—and wound it around a horizontal bar of metal bolted to the deck as Bryn stepped aboard. The boat lurched a second under the transfer of weight, and she mis-stepped and tripped. Lightning-fast, he reached for her, but in her efforts to save herself from hitting the deck she slammed her arm across the instrument console. As she staggered, some of the levers moved.

To her astonishment an engine roared into life.

'What—?' Stunned, she stared at the lever she'd clutched, and then at Bryn as he got there in two swift strides and turned the engine off. Silence echoed around them, broken only by the drumming of her pulse in her ears.

'Why didn't you tell me you'd got the engine going?' she asked, racked by an enormous, unwanted sadness. It had come so quickly, the end of a fragile, beautiful dream.

Had he too not wanted this to end?

One glance at him put paid to that wistful hope. The bone structure of his face had never been so prominent, never seemed so ruthless.

'I didn't,' he said.

Chilled, she shook her head, every uneasy instinct springing into agitated life. 'Then why did it start just then and not when you tried it yesterday?' she asked, watching the play of reflection from the water move across the brutal framework of his face.

He surveyed her with hard eyes that gave nothing away, opaque and green and empty. In a level voice he said, 'Because you turned it on.'

'What?' She blinked, unable to believe that she'd heard correctly.

Bryn looked like something carved out of granite, the only warmth the red gleam summoned by the sun from his tawny hair. Calmly, without inflection, he said, 'I brought us here deliberately. We're staying until I decide to take you back to Fala'isi.'

She spluttered, 'What the hell do you mean?'

'Just that.'

'Are you saying you've *kidnapped* me?'

'No,' he said, eyes steady as they rested on her face. 'You came with me of your own free will so I think the technical term is probably imprisonment.'

By now a whole series of minor questions and queries had jelled. Anger bested fear as adrenalin accelerated her heart, iced her brain. 'You lured me away from New Zealand,' she said, never taking her eyes from his face. 'You made up some specious reason to get me to the hotel, and then you deliberately marooned us here. I gather the boat isn't disabled?'

'No.'

'And the communications system works too?'

'Yes.'

Her knees gave way. Collapsing into one of the chairs, she fought back rage and a bitter, seething disillusionment. When she could trust her voice again she asked, 'Why?'

'If you don't know, you're better off not knowing,' he said with deadly detachment. 'As for luring—no, you came to Longopai on a legitimate mission.'

'A photograph would have been enough to solve that,' she said with bared teeth. She'd been so stupid, allowing herself to be tempted by a week in the islands! Drawing in a ragged breath, she promised, 'But it won't solve your problems when I go to the police once I'm back in New Zealand.'

His smile sent a shudder through her. 'I don't think you will,' he said calmly. 'Who'd believe you? They'd assume that you came to Longopai of your own free will to join me. In fact, they'd know it—why do you think I asked you in front of Cara?'

Gerry said shakily, 'If you don't let me go—today—I'll see you in every court in New Zealand.'

'And if you do that,' he said ruthlessly, 'I'll tell them that you wanted to come, that you wanted to stay, and that your charge is a malicious fabrication because I refused to marry you. It will be my word against yours, because you'll have nobody to back you up.'

'If you think that you can—that you can get away with raping me—'

'Raping you?' His voice roughened, became thick and furious.

Shocked, she realised that she'd almost pushed him into losing control. Gerry wouldn't have believed it to be possible, but his face hardened even further.

However, he pulled back from the brink. 'That wasn't

rape,' he said with calculated indifference. 'I took nothing you weren't willing—eager—to give. I must admit I was flattered to realise that you hadn't slept with anyone for some time. I should have remembered that your friend in Auckland called you unassailable.'

Troy and her drunken ravings, Gerry thought explosively, so angry she could barely articulate the thought.

Gritting her teeth, she said, 'I'd have thought you were sophisticated enough to understand that you can't trust anyone in their cups.'

'Oh, you have a reputation extending well past old friends who ingest mind-altering substances,' he said. 'Didn't you know that, Geraldine? She only said what everyone else says behind your back. The unassailable Gerry! When you smile you make the sun come out, you dazzle with your warmth and your beauty and your laughter, you promise all delight but it's a promise you never keep.'

To the sound of her heart breaking, she asked, 'So what was last night, then?'

His contempt had sliced through the thin shield of her composure, but it was nothing to the wound his smile inflicted. In a deceptively indolent voice he said, 'Oh, you make love like Aphrodite, but it didn't really mean much, did it? You're not grieving now—you're furious.'

Thank God he couldn't read her heart; she'd get out of this with her pride reasonably intact. And because it was so appalling that she should be thinking of pride when every instinct was mourning, she remained silent, lashes lowered as she stared stubbornly at the deck. On her deathbed, she thought, she'd remember the pattern of the boards.

Casually, dismissively, Bryn went on, 'Don't worry, Geraldine, you're quite safe as long as you behave nicely and don't try to run away.' He paused, and then finished, 'I won't sleep with you again.'

'Why did you sleep with me last night?' She tried to speak as easily as he had.

'You were beginning to ask questions,' he said. 'It seemed a good idea to cause a diversion.'

The frail edifice of the night's happiness shattered around her. She ground out, 'What the hell is going on?'

'If you're as innocent as you seem to be, nothing that need concern you,' he said dismissively.

Her hands clenched. Not now, she thought, fighting back the red tide of fury and pain to force her brain into action. After a rapid, painful moment of thought, she said, 'Cara.'

'What about her?'

Think, she commanded. Damn it, you have to think, because he's not going to tell you anything. Perhaps if you make him angry...

Steadying her voice, she said scornfully, 'She's in love with you and you used her to get to me.'

His expression didn't change at all, and when he spoke his voice was amused, almost negligent. 'Cara's dazzled, but her heart won't be dented.'

'God, you're a cold-hearted sod!' The words exploded from her, filled with the fear she refused to accept. 'Why are you keeping me here? What is going on?'

'I can't answer that,' he said, and turned away.

Rage gripped her. 'You mean you won't answer.'

'It doesn't make any difference.'

Finally overwhelmed by anger and pain, she hurled herself forward and hit him, using the variation of street fighting she'd been taught in self-defence lessons years ago.

He was like steel, like rock, but she got in one kidney punch that should have laid him low. He staggered, then rounded on her. Although big men were usually slow, she'd known Bryn was not. However she hadn't been prepared for the lethal speed of his response.

Oddly enough, it gave her some satisfaction. She struck out again, fingers clawing for his eyes, and he parried the blow with his forearm, face blazing with an anger that matched hers.

What followed was an exhausting few minutes of vicious

struggle. Eventually she realised that he wasn't trying to hurt her; he was content to block her every move. She slipped several blows past his guard, but he kept them away from every vulnerable part, until at last, sobbing with frustration, she gave up. Then he locked her wrists together in a grip as tight as it was painful.

'Feel better?' he asked silkily.

As the adrenalin faded into its bitter aftermath, she gained some consolation from the fact of his sweating. Meeting his narrowed, glittering eyes defiantly, she gasped, 'I wish I could kill you.'

'You had a bloody good try. Where did you learn to fight like that?'

'I took lessons years ago.' Her heart threatened to burst through her skin, and the corners of her pareu had loosened, so that she was almost exposed to him. Panting, she said, 'Let me go. I won't try it again.'

'You'd better not.'

He meant it. Shivering, she pulled away, and this time he let her go, watching her while he wiped his hands on the cloth around his hips as though she had contaminated him.

Yanking the ends of her pareu together, she breathed in deeply until she was confident enough of her voice to say, 'For an importer you know how to handle yourself.'

'For a woman who works in high fashion you know some remarkably lethal moves.'

In spite of the heat she felt deathly cold. Swallowing, she said, 'I'd like to go to my room, thank you.'

He went with her—standing guard, she thought with a flash of anger. At her door he said, 'Give me a call when you want to come out and I'll unlock the door.'

In the flat tone of exhaustion she said, 'Let's hope the boat doesn't sink.'

'You should have thought of that before you attacked me.'

Without looking at him, Gerry went inside and listened to the key turn in the lock.

Numbly she walked across to the windows and pushed the glass back. For a moment she wondered whether she should try to get out of a window, but the ones that opened were far too small to take her. Pulling the curtains would stop some of the fresh air, but she couldn't bear the possibility of Bryn checking on her through the window, so she dragged them across.

Then, refusing to think, refusing to feel, she lay down on the big bed and by some kind miracle of sympathetic fate went almost immediately to sleep.

The curtains shimmered gold when she woke, telling her it was late afternoon. She lay for long minutes on the bed, lethargic and aching, trying to work out why Bryn had kidnapped her and was intent on keeping her here.

It had to be something in New Zealand. What? Had Cara's telephone call given him an excuse, or had it been the trigger? Perhaps he'd have suggested a trip in the boat anyway, hiding his purpose with a fake affair.

The thought ached physically through her. But it could wait; she'd deal with it when she knew what was going on.

Cara was the only link, and Gerry's decision to go back to New Zealand had precipitated this abduction, if abduction it could be called when the abductee had co-operated so eagerly.

No, she wouldn't think of that. Please God, Honor would soon arrive back from wherever she'd been to look after the agency, and Maddie—

Maddie.

Gerry's heart stopped. Maddie had overdosed on heroin. Was that—could that be—the link? Had Cara rung Bryn to tell him about it?

No. Why would she? And what would it mean to him?

She could have, Gerry's rational brain said relentlessly.

Or Bryn could have monitored the calls Gerry made in her cabaña after she'd left him.

An importer with a legal business and impeccable credentials as a businessman—a man like Bryn Falconer—would find it quite easy to set up an illicit organisation to ship in drugs.

Nausea made Gerry gag, but she rinsed out her mouth and washed her face and sat down again. If that unscrupulous importer could persuade a credulous young girl like Cara, who had contacts with people going overseas, that he needed to bring stuff in without Customs knowing—then perhaps the agency could be used as a distributing point.

An island like Longopai would be very useful too, she thought, remembering the trading vessel he had bought for the islanders so that they wouldn't be dependent on the schedules of others.

Such a man could probably persuade Cara to store the stuff in her house; grim logic reminded Gerry he'd wanted Cara's landlady away from Auckland.

No, it was impossible. She'd been watching too many late-night television shows.

Yet here she was, caged in a boat on the Pacific, an almost-willing prisoner who'd swallowed everything Bryn told her because she was attracted to him. Oh, she'd been a fool!

Common sense should have told her that it was highly unlikely—to say the least!—that every system on a boat like *Starchaser* would fail together. Yet she'd been so mesmerised by Bryn's physical magnetism that she'd swallowed his sketchy explanation hook, line and sinker.

A blast of fury surged through her, was suppressed; it clouded the brain. What she needed was clear-headed logic. Unclenching her teeth, she wooed calmness.

From now on she wasn't going to take anything for granted. 'Think,' she muttered. 'Stop wailing and think!'

Could Cara be so criminally naive as to fall in with a scheme like that? Probably not, but she was easily dazzled—and Gerry had first-hand experience of just how plausible Bryn could be.

No, it was utterly ridiculous! Gerry got to her feet and paced through the stateroom, shaking her head. She was spinning tales out of shadows.

She had absolutely no proof, nothing but the wildest speculations.

Yet Bryn had lied about the boat, and kept her prisoner. And he'd made love to her because she'd asked questions—what questions? Was it when she asked who he'd been talking to? He must have been using the radio. Humiliation stung through her but she ignored it.

Also, he certainly hadn't been fooling when he'd locked the door behind her.

Unless he was a psychopath he must have good reasons for his actions.

Psychopath or drug importer—both seemed so unlikely she couldn't deal with them. Yet she would have to accept that she might well be in danger—in such danger that her only hope of saving herself lay in pretending she was the stupid piece of fluff he clearly thought her to be.

Adrenalin brought her upright, but before it had time to develop into full-blown terror a flash of memory made her sink back down again. The first time they'd met, Bryn had held a baby in his arms, and smiled at it with tenderness and awe and a fierce protectiveness.

That had been when she fell in love with him, Gerry thought now. Could a man who'd looked at a child like that cold-bloodedly sleep with a woman and then murder her?

Her heart said no, but she'd already found out she couldn't trust that unwary organ. She'd have to work on the assumption that Bryn Falconer was exactly that sort of man.

She rubbed a shaking hand across her forehead. Why did he need to keep her out of the way now?

Because Maddie had overdosed?

No, it was too far-fetched, too much like some thriller. She was overwrought, and so stressed by his betrayal that her mind was running riot.

But why else would he be keeping her here incommunicado? Obviously he hadn't booked her plane seat to New Zealand, so no one except Cara and Jill were expecting her. With bitter irony, Gerry realised that he'd probably rung Cara and reassured her, giving her some excellent reason why Gerry wasn't coming home. A tropical fever perhaps, she thought wearily. Not dangerous, but debilitating. And perhaps he'd asked Cara to tell Jill that everything was all right.

Gerry tried to remember whether she'd told him about her conversation with the booker. No, she wouldn't have, but if he'd monitored her calls from Longopai he'd know Jill wouldn't be sending off search parties.

He really didn't have anything to worry about. The islanders were his—if he asked them not to speak they wouldn't.

And if he wanted to kill her then he'd probably find a way to get rid of Cara too.

Panic clawed at her gut. She rested her hands on her diaphragm and concentrated on breathing, slow and easy, in and out, in and out, until her racing brain slowed and the terror had subsided.

Ridiculous; it was all ridiculous. This was Bryn who made love like a dark angel, Bryn who'd been gentle when she needed gentleness, fierce when she needed ferocity, Bryn who had made her laugh and talked to her with intelligence and a rare, understated compassion.

Unfortunately history was full of women who had been betrayed by the men they'd loved, men they'd given up everything for.

So she was going to take any chance she could to get away. She'd never forgive herself if she didn't do something to protect Cara.

First, she'd try to use the communications system and send out an SOS.

If she got out of this unscathed, she promised herself grimly, she'd not only take those Maori classes, she'd do a course in maritime navigation and communications.

Or perhaps it would be simpler never to set foot off dry land again.

CHAPTER TEN

WHEN Bryn opened the door some hours later Gerry was sitting on her bed, hands folded in her lap, face carefully blank, while the flicker of fear burnt brightly in her mind.

'You look like a good little girl,' he said, a smile just touching the corners of his mouth.

Gerry's heart leapt frantically. No, she thought gratefully, she couldn't believe he had any connection to the wild concoction of ideas she'd dreamed up.

'I always try to please kidnappers,' she said with a slight snap.

His mouth tightened. 'Come out and have a drink.'

He looked dangerous, but not murderous. Still buoyed by that spurt of relief, she knew that of course he wasn't a murderer! He had, however, lied to her and abducted her, and he wouldn't tell her why.

So she had to work on the assumption that he was up to something that was not for her good.

Getting to her feet, she picked up the letter she'd written to keep her mind from tearing off into ever wilder shores of conjecture, then preceded him into the main cabin.

Once there, she said, 'I've written to Lacey. I'd like to send it to her if you have her address.'

'Send it to the hotel and ask them to forward it,' he said coolly.

'It's not sealed. Do you want to read it?' She held it out to him.

His brows drew together. 'Stop pushing,' he commanded softly.

But she couldn't. 'I haven't written anything that might lead her to think I'm in dire danger.'

'Keep on like that, and you might be. If you send it to the hotel they'll make sure Lacey gets it.'

Gerry said chattily, 'I made her promise to contact a doctor when she gets back home. I thought I'd better remind her of it just in case I go missing.'

'You won't go missing,' he said between his teeth. 'How did you extract a promise like that from her?'

'I threatened to tell her parents. Oh, I didn't say so, but she knew I would. She wants to stop; the bulimia terrifies her but she's also determined not to put any weight on. She needs professional help, and I more or less blackmailed her into seeing someone she trusts when she gets home.'

He said nothing, and she went on abruptly, 'I'm beginning to wonder whether there might not be some truth in what you said about magazines sending all the wrong messages.'

'Guilty conscience, Geraldine?'

She shrugged moodily, trying to sound and look normal, trying to reassure herself that a man who worried about the messages high fashion was sending to young women couldn't possibly be a drug peddler. 'No. The magazine I worked for concentrated on style rather than fashion, and we did a lot with models who weren't size eights. As for the agency, we represent all sorts—character as well as fashion—and I can assure you that none of our models are anorexic or bulimic.'

But one was a drug addict. Just how much did she know about the models?

Swiftly she went on, 'Lacey worries me. She's big-boned, the sort of build with no middle ground between gaunt and voluptuous. She's also bitterly unhappy with her stepmother, and I gathered that her mother doesn't want her living with her and her new husband. I don't entirely believe that the fashion business is to blame for the increase in eating disorders. There are millions of women throughout the world who read fashion magazines, and although they're nothing like the models they're happy with their lot.'

Bryn walked across to the drinks fridge. 'I know.'

He caught her surprised glance. A cynical lift of his mouth made him look suddenly older. 'Wine?' he asked.

'No, thank you. Something with fruit in it.'

He poured her pineapple juice, and lime and soda for himself. If he'd chosen beer she might have had a chance to try and get him drunk.

Hardly. Bryn Falconer was a very controlled man; it was difficult to imagine him drinking to excess.

Silence stretched between them. Refusing to show how intimidated she was, Gerry sipped her drink. Outside the sun had set; as the darkness thickened a bird flying overhead gave a strange, wild cry, and she only just prevented herself from jumping.

'Relax,' he said, something like irritation flicking through his voice. 'I told you before, you're in no danger. Stop looking at me as though you expect me to leap on you.'

'I'm not accustomed to being held prisoner,' she returned crisply. 'It makes me angry.'

'You're not just angry,' he said. 'You're scared.'

Damn. She made her muscles respond in a smile, packed though it was with irony. 'You must forgive me, but in spite of all your protestations about not wanting to harm me, you are holding me here for reasons I'm not allowed to know. I think a certain amount of wariness is normal in such situations. Of course I *believe* you when you say I'm safe,' she finished, her voice dripping polite sarcasm. 'How long will I be forced to stay here?'

'Until I'm told it's safe to let you go.'

So he wasn't doing this on his own. Well, she'd realised that there had to be other people in it with him, whatever *it* was!

Feeling her way, she said, 'A week? A month? A year?'

But of course he wasn't goaded into revealing anything. 'Until I let you go,' he repeated levelly, his face impassive, as though they'd never looked at each other with naked lust, never made love, never slept a long night in each other's arms.

'What excuse did you give Cara for my not coming back?'

'I told her you had a very mild case of dengue fever. She said that you weren't to worry, she and Jill would cope,' he told her, and before she had a chance to say anything more went on, 'I'll get dinner.'

He'd cooked steak, and served it with potatoes and taro leaves cooked in coconut milk. Gerry had no appetite, but she forced as much as she could down because she wasn't going to weaken herself by starving.

After the meal she said, 'I'd like to go back to the cabin now.'

Hot anger glittered in Bryn's gaze, was immediately extinguished. 'Of course,' he said courteously.

So Gerry sat in the small room, nerves taut, and listened to the sound of the waves on the reef. Towards ten o'clock she heard his voice drift in through the open windows. It was impossible to make out individual words, but from his tone—crisp, businesslike, resolute—it was clear that he was using the radio.

She was never going to trust any other man, no matter how attractive she found him and how tenderly he looked at babies.

Thoughts prowled through her mind, rattling the bars and poking hideous faces as the slow tropical night wheeled through its cycle, splendid, indifferent, majestically beautiful. Lying tense and fully-clothed on the bed, Gerry spent hours trying to convince herself that the man who had made love to her with such fiery tenderness couldn't possibly want to harm her.

Dawn came as a surprise. Yawning, she rubbed her eyes and realised that somehow she'd managed to fall asleep.

A glance in the mirror revealed dark circles under her eyes, and sallow, colourless skin. Hastily she showered before making up with every ounce of skill and care she could call on, not satisfied until her face gazed back at her— smooth and unmarked by betrayal, the sleepy eyes and full mouth delicately enhanced so that no one could guess how much time it had taken to manufacture that discreet, inconspicuous mask.

She dressed in white linen trousers and a muted silk shirt in her favourite shades of blue and green, slid her narrow feet into blue sandals, and straightened her shoulders and lifted her chin. With her best model gait she walked across to the door.

It was unlocked. Hardly daring to breathe, she slipped through it.

Bryn looked up from the galley. 'Good morning,' he said, scanning her with half-closed eyes that sent a shiver from the top of her head to the base of her spine, so masculine and appreciative was that swift, hot glance. It disappeared in the length of a blink; he lifted his brows and said easily, 'Ah, the exquisite, sophisticated, aloof Ms Dacre once more! It's almost a pity; I've grown to like the slightly tousled Geraldine who lurks beneath the cosmetics.'

Smiling, showing her teeth, she murmured, 'How sweet.'

He laughed. 'Come and have some breakfast.'

No, she thought hopefully, whatever the reason he kept her here, it couldn't possibly be because he was smuggling drugs. That had been a fevered figment of her imagination; he couldn't look at her like that, or tease like that—couldn't *laugh* like that—and wish her any harm.

With a cautiously lifting heart, she sat down at the table and began to eat.

He didn't lock her into her cabin again; as though they'd silently negotiated a truce they tidied the boat and repaired to the cockpit, sitting out of the sun. Bryn read what looked like business papers from a locked briefcase, and Gerry tried to concentrate on a book.

With very little success. A volatile cocktail of emotions—raw fury and desolation and pride mixed with a persistent, stubborn hope—washed through her like rollers pounding the shore. Ignore the hope, she told herself, it will weaken you. Polish up that pride.

And look for an opportunity to get to the instrument console and radio for help, even though you have no idea how to use it.

However, he'd placed himself between her and the console, and during the long morning he made sure she didn't have a chance to get near it.

The sun was high in the sky when something beeped from the panel. Bryn looked up. 'Would you mind going below?' he asked pleasantly.

'Not at all,' Gerry replied with steely composure, gathering up the unread book as she got to her feet.

Of course she couldn't settle; clutching the book, she stood in the main cabin and stared blindly through the windows while Bryn's voice echoed in her ears.

Should she be frightened?

No.

However hard she tried to see him as a criminal, she couldn't. Oh, she could imagine Bryn killing a man in self-defence, but even in her most paranoid fears she hadn't been able to be afraid of him. A deep-seated instinct told her he was a man with his own strict code of honour.

Her lips stretched in a painful, wry smile. In spite of everything her foolish heart trusted him. Nevertheless that same organ gave an enormous jump when he appeared in the doorway, brows drawn together, face grim.

'Well?' she demanded.

He came down the last step. 'Tell me about your partner in the agency,' he commanded.

'Honor?' Totally bewildered, Gerry stared at him. 'What's happened? Is she all right?'

'As far as I know she's fine,' he said. 'How long have you known her? Where did you meet her?'

She asked, 'Do you know whether a model called Maddie Ingram is all right? She was in hospital.'

It was a test. If he knew about Maddie, he knew too much.

He paused a second before saying, 'She's recovering.'

A clutch of terror diluted Gerry's relief. Yet her voice

stayed steady when she asked, 'Why do you want to know about Honor?'

'Because it's important.' The relentless note in his voice warned her that she wasn't going to be able to stall.

Feeling oddly disconnected, she said slowly, 'She used to be a model—I've known her for years.'

'Is she a friend?'

She gave him a startled look but could read nothing from the harsh face or hooded eyes.

'Not exactly a friend,' she answered slowly. 'We get on well together, and she's an excellent partner.'

'What made you decide to go in with her?'

He sounded like a policeman—polite, determined, relentless. The hairs on the back of her neck stood up. 'After my father died I was restless, and when the magazine I worked for was taken over, and the new owners put in an editor who took it down a path I despise, I started looking around for another job. Honor had just broken up with the man she'd been living with.'

Drugs, she recalled sickly. He'd been a heroin addict. She cast a swift glance at Bryn's stone-featured face and continued, 'He'd run through all her money and she was desperate. The only thing she knew was modelling, so she suggested we open an agency. At the time it seemed a good way of getting over my grief. A model agency is the next best thing to chaos that you've ever come across—you don't have time to think.'

'How was the agency set up?'

'On a shoestring. Neither of us had any money—what we did have were contacts. And I have a reputation for seeing promise in unlikely people.'

'Who actually runs the agency?'

Gerry said crisply, 'In an agency as small as ours we can all do everything. We've got bookers, of course—they organise the models' bookings—but Honor and I do almost everything else, and we take the responsibility for planning careers.'

'All right,' he cut in. 'Who deals with the finances?'

Frowning, Gerry said, 'We have an accountant.'

'Who is sleeping with Honor McKenzie.'

She looked up sharply. There had been no inflection in his tone, but something warned her that she wasn't going to like what was coming. 'I hope not,' she said just as brusquely. 'He's married to a very nice woman.'

'He's been your partner's lover since before the agency opened.'

Gerry said quietly, 'I didn't know that.'

'Do you know where Honor was when Cara rang you in a panic about Maddie Ingram?'

Who the *hell* was he? Or rather, *what* was he? He certainly didn't sound like your average rich importer. And where was this all heading? Chilled by nameless fear, Gerry shook her head. 'Cara said she couldn't contact her, but that's not unusual. She takes the occasional long weekend off.'

In an expressionless voice he told her, 'She was in Tahiti.'

Tahiti? Six hours away from New Zealand by air? Her expression must have revealed Gerry's astonishment, but she said evenly, 'I don't understand why this is important.'

'She was meeting an emissary from a Colombian cocaine-trafficking cartel.'

Gerry's jaw dropped.

Calmly, mercilessly, Bryn went on, 'Colombians made the big time with cocaine but now they're moving into heroin—it's easier to transport and yields far higher profits. In New Zealand, what heroin comes in—and that's not been much until recently—has been sourced in Asia.'

'From the Golden Triangle,' Gerry said dully. She'd read about the wild region on the border of Thailand and Myanmar where drug lords ruled an empire based on misery.

Although she knew now what he was going to tell her, she was gripped by an overwhelming relief, a giddy sense of being reprieved from something too dreadful to contemplate because her suspicions of Bryn were baseless.

'Yes. The Colombians want this traffic; using New Zealand as a staging post, they can move into Australia and Asia.' Sources say they have over forty thousand acres of opium poppy under cultivation, and they're planting more. They're also aggressive marketers. Their product is cheaper and purer than the Asian stuff, and they're "double-breasting"—offering a free sample of heroin to each buyer of cocaine.'

She said, 'You think there's a connection between Maddie's overdose and Honor.'

He frowned. 'There's certainly a link with the agency.'

'How do you know?'

'There have been whispers about the agency for a year or so, but nothing tangible, nothing the police could put a finger on. However, Maddie told a friend she had a contact there, and the friend, thank God, told Maddie's brother. He went to the police, and your agency has been under investigation since then.'

'How do I know that you're not lying, that this isn't some elaborate scam?' Gerry couldn't believe it. She knew Honor much better than she knew him, and she'd never suspected her partner of any connection with drug-dealing. 'And why did you stop me from going back to New Zealand?'

'The police asked me to keep you away from the agency for as long as possible.'

'Why?'

'They were still not entirely convinced that you weren't part of the drug ring.' He spoke unemotionally, but she realised he was watching her with an intense, unnerving concentration, dispassionate and intimidating. 'Although they had a search warrant they needed time to get into your computers and drag everything out. They've been there since half an hour after Cara rang you.'

'I see,' she said in a stifled monotone. Thoughts barged around her head, colliding, melding in turmoil. She drew a deep breath and said harshly, 'Why do the police think Honor had something to do with Maddie's OD? And how—how do you know who she met in Tahiti? You can prove that, I assume?'

'She's been under surveillance, and, yes, it can be proved.'

Sweat sprang out across her skin in great beads as she closed her eyes, but blocking him out didn't help. 'Who are you? Apart from being an importer?'

Eyes as cold as quartz, he told her, 'I'm not—I lied to you. I own a construction company. We do projects all around the Pacific Rim, and the company was used in a smuggling racket some years ago. I worked closely with Customs and the police to get to the bottom of that, so I have contacts within each department.'

Frowning, Gerry asked, 'And how did you get mixed up with this?'

After an infinitesimal pause he answered, 'I'm a good friend of Peter Ingram, Maddie's brother. He contacted me a couple of months ago, after he'd found out she was back on heroin. He had to leave for Turkestan and I promised I'd keep an eye on her. I also went to the police. They contacted me a few weeks ago to see if I could get you out of the way for a few days.'

'So you set out to find some dimwitted person with a connection to the agency and picked up Cara, who led you to me.' Her voice was brittle, as brittle as her heart.

His mouth tightened but he said evenly, 'Yes. You were the most likely suspect.'

'Why?' Her emotions were lost in a hollow emptiness.

'A tip-off.'

She stared at him. 'A tip-off?' she said numbly. 'Who from?'

He was still watching her with cool, unsparing assessment. 'A long-time drug user. The police suspect that he mistook you for Honor. Or she might have used your name occasionally.'

Sinking down onto the sofa, she looked down at her feet.

Nausea made her swallow. Bryn had believed this; he'd been sure that she was a prime mover in this trade, and he'd slept with her, made love to her...

It was only marginally less shattering than if he'd been the dealer of death. Her throat ached with tears, tears she'd never be able to shed. She said, 'And on that basis, a tip from a known drug user, you assumed that I ran a drug ring.'

'There were other factors. When the police began investigating, a trail led them to a Swiss bank account, supposedly set up by you.'

With a sense of complete unreality, Gerry noticed that her hands were trembling. Sweat collected across her shoulders, ran the length of her back. Her arid throat prevented her from speaking until she'd swallowed again, and even then her voice emerged thin and shaken. She could discern nothing in Bryn's hard face, nothing in his tone, to tell her whether he believed this or not.

'No,' she said.

'It certainly gave credence to the tip-off,' he said neutrally.

Had Honor done this? Gerry had always been reasonably confident about her judgement of character until then; now she realised that the woman she'd worked with and trusted could have plotted to send her to prison, to ruin her life. She shook her head.

'It made sense,' Bryn went on with grim persistence. 'Although your father had indulged you all your life, his insistence on paying back his creditors left you penniless.'

'I had a salary,' she flared.

'Peanuts to what you'd been accustomed to. Before he divested himself to pay off his creditors your father was a rich man.'

Gerry said tautly, 'My father stopped supporting me when I left university, and since then I've lived off my income. I agreed wholly with him when he decided to pay back the money his manager had taken.'

'It seemed likely that you might look for a way to up

your income to that level again. Also, you'd done a lot of travelling when you were with the magazine, especially in Asia and the Pacific. Plenty of chances to make contacts there. And then there was the friend I saw you eating lunch with the day I met you. She'd taken something.'

'She'd had less than a glass of wine. Troy's very susceptible to alcohol—it makes her drunk so quickly she can't even eat a sherry trifle.' With an effort that took all of her nervous energy, she steadied her voice. 'So when we made love you really thought that I was running a smuggling ring. Not only that, but that I was introducing my models to heroin.'

'By then I was almost convinced that you were innocent.'

His impersonal, judicial tone fired her anger to fury—a fury mixed with weary disillusion.

'Almost.' She straightened her spine. 'Go on,' she said tonelessly. 'Tell me how you decided that it was Honor.'

'You don't seem surprised,' he observed shrewdly.

Slowly Gerry said, 'I am—but not shocked. In some ways she's surprisingly amoral, so perhaps I should have wondered if that extended into other areas of her life. But she didn't try to fiddle the books—I learned from my father's experience, and I go over the records regularly.'

'You went over the records she wanted you to see. There were others, but she kept her illegal activities totally separate from the agency.'

'Except for Maddie,' she said bitterly.

He shrugged. 'Except for Maddie. Nevertheless, the police realised that, in spite of the tip-off, Honor McKenzie had just as many chances as you to travel, she had as little money as you, and she'd also lived with a man who was deep in the drug culture.'

'She isn't a user,' Gerry said, adding wearily, 'at least, I don't think she is.'

'She isn't, and neither is her lover, who actually set this whole thing up. The people who sell rarely are. They know what damage their wares cause.'

'If there was a bank account in my name, how did the police decide that it was Honor who organised the trade, not me?' Her cool voice hid, she hoped, the intense desolation that racked her.

'It all seemed just a little too pat—especially when it was discovered that the accountant and Honor were lovers. He was a suspect in a fraud case five years ago—they couldn't pin anything on him, but the Fraud Squad were convinced that he was not only guilty but the organiser of the scam. A month ago your accounting department hired a clerk, an undercover agent who's a computer expert. If you know what you're doing you can find anything that's ever been on a computer, even if it's been dumped in the trash. She was surprised to find security so tight in your accounting department, but she dug away discreetly, only to be even more surprised to find a not too difficult trail leading to a Swiss bank account—in your name.'

Gerry licked dry lips. 'I see,' she said quietly. 'You mean the agency has been used to launder money?'

'No, but the agency's computers had been used to organise it all. Apparently by you. And that increased the police suspicions, because the trail was a little too clear, a little too obvious. So they began looking into Honor's affairs, and they found that she'd gone to Thailand earlier this year, and while she was there she'd met a couple of extremely unsavoury characters. The New Zealand police liaise very closely with the Thai drug squad, and they'd been watching these men.'

Thank heavens for suspicious police. Gerry's shoulders ached with the effort it took to keep them straight.

To her astonishment Bryn asked, 'Do you want a drink—a cup of tea, something?'

Her stomach roiled at the prospect. 'No thanks. Go on.'

'Honor has been living just above her income; she seems to be taking great care not to exceed it by enough to cause suspicion. But even then you weren't entirely in the clear. They were certain Honor was guilty, but your status was problematical. She and her lover might well have intended to use you as a scapegoat, hence the nice clear trail to the Swiss account.'

'So the police decided that you should sniff around much more closely,' she said, not even trying to inject some emotion into the words. 'What a pity I'm not good at pillow talk.'

Although green fire smouldered in the depths of his eyes, his voice remained level. 'In the end they decided to apply a little pressure.'

'How?'

'You were got out of the way and put in a situation where any calls could be monitored.' His voice was hard. 'Honor was contacted by someone who told her he could sell heroin at a cut rate—much better heroin than she was getting from Asia. He sent her a sample which had been tagged.'

'Tagged?'

'Treated so that it is easily identifiable. She didn't even try to contact you; instead, she and the accountant took off for Tahiti after they'd sold the heroin on. It was traced through several people, including the person who'd named you. He's been taken into custody, and he talked enough to convince the police he'd never met the woman he called Gerry. The accountant and Honor were arrested half an hour ago as they landed from Tahiti.'

Gerry couldn't bear to look at him, couldn't bear to think of Honor, peddling beauty and death. Reining herself in, she asked, 'It still isn't conclusive proof that I'm in the clear?'

He frowned. 'The police have been through your affairs with a fine-tooth comb, and nothing but the tip-off connects you to the smuggling. You live within your income, you have no secret assets, and the hidden bank account has been examined by the Swiss—although it was set up under your name, the beneficiaries turned out to be Honor and the accountant. That's proof enough, Geraldine.'

'Why?' Gerry asked harshly. She should be relieved, but

she was too shattered to feel anything. 'What made her do it?'

'She's in it for the money.' Contempt seared the words. 'She met the accountant, and the two of them set it up; you were the perfect scapegoat.'

'So you did your duty as a good citizen and got me out of the way while they investigated Honor. I admire your dedication to the cause.'

He shrugged. 'By then I was as certain as anyone could be without proof that you were in the clear.'

'But you needed that proof,' she said, her quiet comment hiding, she hoped, the pain behind it. 'And you made love to me to stop me from making any connections. You must think I'm a total fool. I must *be* a total fool.'

'I made love to you because I couldn't help myself,' he said roughly.

Why did he lie? Did it matter? Driven by the need to escape, to lick her wounds in private, she said, 'It seems you make a habit of using women. First Cara, then me—'

He said ferociously, 'Will you stop saying that? I haven't even kissed Cara, and as for you—doesn't it tell you something that when I should have kept you at arm's length I couldn't wait to get into bed with you?'

'It tells me that—' She stopped, twisting her head. 'What's that? It sounds like a plane.'

Bryn swore under his breath, but didn't try to stop her when she brushed past him and ran up the steps. The seaplane headed towards them and came in slowly, settling into the lagoon in twin feathers of spray.

Bryn said, 'I called him up half an hour ago, but he said he'd be at least an hour.'

'You can't trust anyone nowadays, can you?' Gerry said bitterly.

'I'll get your luggage,' he said tightly, disappearing down the steps.

Biting her lip, Gerry walked across to the railing, watching through a mist of tears as the plane taxied to a stop. What had she expected? Making love to her had been hardly honourable, but then, he had done it for the good of the country, she thought tiredly.

And she was not in love with him.

Not even one tiny bit.

It was a silent trip in the dinghy to the plane. All Gerry had to rely on now was her dignity. She forced a smile for the pilot and his hairy, enthusiastic co-pilot, who barked a greeting and had to be restrained from hurtling into the lagoon. Without hearing the pleasantries Bryn and the pilot exchanged, she clambered in.

Bryn looked up, green eyes burning in the emphatic framework of his dark, autocratic face. 'Goodbye, Geraldine,' he said, and expertly backed the dinghy away, rowing steadily towards the *Starchaser*.

She couldn't summon a reply; instead she nodded and settled back into her seat.

'Put your seatbelt on,' the pilot yelled.

She did up the clasp and turned her head resolutely away, watching the island skim past until the engine noise altered and they lifted above the vivid lagoon. As soon as they were in the air she allowed herself to wipe her eyes and blow her nose, and watched steadfastly as the water fell away beneath them and the bright, feathery crowns of the coconut palms dwindled into a fringe within the protective white line of the reef, and then were left behind.

CHAPTER ELEVEN

'ALL right,' Gerry said with a sigh, 'let's call it a day.'

Troy covered a yawn. 'It's been a long one,' she said with a grimace, looking at the cluttered circular table with its central rack of files.

Gerry got to her feet and stretched. 'Oh, well, it's over now.'

The past six months had been horrendous, with Honor in prison awaiting trial, and then the trial itself, culminating in long sentences for both her and her lover. Gerry had been appalled to discover how cleverly the whole operation had been managed. Honor had targeted the rich and the famous—people who'd wanted to avoid any sleaze or violence or danger.

The agency had been thoroughly compromised, but although they had lost models, many had stuck by Gerry. Which was surprising, as Honor's defence had suggested with infinite delicacy that Gerry had been the prime mover in the heroin ring and that Honor had been framed.

Gerry thought drearily that her models' loyalty had been virtually the only good thing about these last six months.

No, that was untrue. She'd learned enough basic Maori at night classes to make herself understood, and Lacey hadn't vomited for three months. She and the Australian girl kept in close touch with e-mail, and it certainly sounded as though Lacey was getting her life together.

Abruptly Gerry said, 'I'm going to sell the agency.'

Troy stared. 'Why? You've worked like a slave to control all the damage, and now that things are going smoothly again you want to leave. It doesn't make sense. What will you do?'

It was impossible to tell her the real reason—that Gerry was heartsick for a man who hadn't been near her since, grim-faced and impervious, he'd watched her leave him. Bryn hadn't appeared in any of the court proceedings; for all she knew, he could have disappeared off the face of the earth.

She said, 'I'm going to have a holiday. And I think I might learn to cook. Properly.'

Troy's mouth opened, then closed on her unspoken comment. After a moment, she nodded. 'Good idea. And after you've learned to cook properly—what then?'

'I'm going to write a column for one of the magazines—personal style, to thine own self be true, where to shop for good, elegant, stylish clothes that suit and don't break the budget—that sort of thing. Under a pseudonym, of course. The editors think—and I agree—that it would be better to lie low for a while until the stink from this has died down, if it ever does. Mud sticks.'

Troy said briskly, 'Don't be an idiot. Anyone who knows you knows you had nothing to do with Honor and her rotten get-rich-quick scheme.' She paused before asking, 'Are you going to be able to earn enough to live on?'

'I should get a decent sum for the agency. It's worth quite a bit, so I'll pay off the mortgage on the house, repay the bank loan that I took out to buy Honor's share of the agency, and invest any money left over. I won't be able to live on that, but as well as the magazine column, I've been thinking about going back to journalism—freelancing.' She gave a wry smile. 'There'll be enough variety in that to stop me getting bored. I used to enjoy writing articles, and I was good at it.'

'You were brilliant at it,' Troy said, eyeing her thoughtfully. 'I think it's a wonderful idea. Have you got a buyer for the agency?'

'The first person with the money,' Gerry answered cynically. 'No, it'll have to be someone I trust. I haven't got it back into running order to sell it to anyone I don't like. I probably haven't thanked you for coming in as assistant and general dogsbody, either. Honestly, Troy, it's made all the difference.'

'I've loved doing it.'

'How does Damon feel about it?'

Her friend set two pens carefully down on the table. 'At first he hated it, and whined about how bad a wife and mother I am, even though the new nanny is working out brilliantly—the kids love her, and she's so good with them.' She picked up a pen and fiddled with it. 'Anyway, it doesn't matter what he thinks. I've left him.'

Gerry landed limply in the chair beside her. 'Oh,' she said inadequately.

Troy flushed, but held her head high. 'And it's not because he's having an affair with one of his executives, either. I'd decided before I knew about that. I just looked at him and thought, Would anyone who really loved me treat me the way he does? And I thought, No, if you love someone you want them to be happy, instead of making them miserable as sin. So I got my lawyer to draw up a separation agreement. Damon's flounced off to live with his dark-haired, clever girlfriend, and the kids and I are in the house with the nanny.'

'I'm sorry,' Gerry said. Sorry, she meant, for shattered illusions and broken dreams, not sorry that Damon had gone. 'Why didn't you tell me?'

Troy looked self-conscious. 'Well, you've been so busy with the agency, and so worried about the court case, I didn't want to add to your woes. And I needed to do this on my own. I've always turned to you and cried all over you and generally leaned on you; I thought it was about time I grew up and made some decisions for myself, and carried through on them.'

'You've certainly done that,' Gerry said, feeling oddly abandoned.

Troy shook her head. 'Yes, well, it hasn't been easy,' she admitted, 'but really I've known ever since we got married that I'd been a fool—I just didn't want to admit it. You know me, stubborn as hell. This job has been a lifesaver, and I've loved it.' She looked around the office with its posters of models on the walls, its air of being in a contin-

ual state of chaos, and said, 'And I'd have to talk it over
with my financial advisers, but I'd like to buy the agency
very much. I know you bought Honor out—she hasn't any
other claim on it, has she?'

'No,' Gerry said shortly. She'd gone to the finance company expecting to be turned down, but it had been no problem, and Honor, needing the cash for lawyers, had been
eager to be rid of her share.

'Good.' Troy put the pen down. She looked eager and
excited, more like the woman who'd been a very successful
model than the overwrought wife who'd wept in the restaurant six months ago. 'Do you remember Sunny Josephs,
who used to be booker for me in the days when I was
setting the catwalks on fire? She went off to Chicago just
after I married, and did really well there, but she wants to
come home. She wrote to me a couple of months ago and
asked if there was something she could buy into here. There
wasn't at the time, but if she's interested in coming in as
my partner, it would be perfect. She knows more about the
industry than anyone else, and having her here would give
me more time with the kids.'

'It sounds ideal,' Gerry said.

'It does, doesn't it?' Her friend smiled. 'OK, then, I'll
get my financial person to talk to yours.'

Troy had worked hard, earning trust and respect from the
models. Her background had helped, but it was her driving
desire to succeed that would make her a success. If she
wanted to put the small fortune she'd earned from her days
as a model into the agency, she'd do well.

Gerry drove home through a late summer dusk, enjoying
the incandescent colours of sunset staining the western sky.
Auckland had wound down for the day, but there were still
too many cars on the roads and plenty of people on the
streets. Through her windows floated that indescribable
mixture of flowers and car fumes and salt and barbecues—
the scents of Auckland in summer.

But in her heart it was always winter, and even as she
scoffed at herself for being melodramatic she accepted that

the interlude with Bryn had altered her life, changed something basic in her soul.

She couldn't have fallen in love so quickly, so what she felt for him had to be sheer, teeth-clenching frustration, an intense, unsatisfied desire. If they'd had a torrid affair she'd be restless by now, seeking ways to be free of him without hurting him.

Turning into her gate, she hit the button for the garage and watched the door fold upwards. As she nudged into place beside the empty space where Cara's sporty little model usually sat, she smiled. After a couple of edgy months pining for Bryn, Cara had found herself a boyfriend. Simon played professional rugby and had been picked for the All Blacks, New Zealand's national team.

It had to be true love, Gerry had decided, because although he was a dear, and very intelligent, with a degree in history, he was a far cry from the handsome models and television stars Cara had preferred before him. In spite of this, Cara seemed totally besotted, and although Simon viewed his love with a slightly sardonic gaze, he clearly loved her deeply. Gerry hoped it would last, especially as Cara was talking about moving in with him.

Her new housemate wasn't home either. Improbably named Alfred, he was six feet two of impossibly gorgeous male with shoulders as wide as barn doors. He drove a beat-up Falcon with rusty doors and a hood that rattled, in which he'd been living until Gerry offered him a room and bed, and was headed for super-stardom as a model. So far he'd stuck close to home because his father was ill, but it wouldn't be long before he was snapped up by the overseas market.

She'd miss him. Not only was he funny and a good cook, but he'd provided eager muscle when she'd remodelled the garden that spring.

The prospect of finding another housemate was depressing. But then, she thought, walking between banks of cosmos to the door, everything depressed her this golden summer. Since she'd flown away from an unnamed atoll and left Bryn Falconer behind, life had seemed too much trouble.

She'd hoped that when she sent a carefully selected folder of photographs of hats for the Longopai islanders to copy he might contact her, but he hadn't, unless you counted a formal, perfectly phrased letter written by his secretary to thank her for her efforts on the islanders' behalf.

Even now that Gerry had secured the future of her models and cleared her name as far as it could be cleared, and was confident the agency would be in good hands, she couldn't summon much enthusiasm for either a holiday or her latest venture into journalism.

She stooped to smell a heavy peach and yellow Abraham Derby rose, losing herself in its intense, heady fragrance. As she stood up and walked towards the front verandah a blackbird, deciding she was an imminent threat to avian life, flew screaming across the lawn towards the hedge.

'Oh, grow up!' Gerry told it crisply, and bent to examine the round, glossy leaves of her Chatham Island forget-me-nots. It was a gamble, growing them this close to the equator, but given the right place they could thrive even in Auckland's warm, humid, maritime climate. These ones looked all right so far, but getting them through the summer would be tricky.

As a car stopped outside the hedge a latent, atavistic intuition pulled her skin taut. Every sense on full alert, she straightened, staring at the house, unable to swivel around.

'Geraldine.'

How had she known? She hadn't seen him, certainly hadn't heard him, and yet from the moment the car drew to a halt she'd known it was Bryn.

Gathering her inner resources, she slowly turned. As he came towards her, her heart contracted fiercely, squeezing her emotions into one solid, unreachable ball. 'Hello, Bryn,' she said quietly. 'How are you?'

'I'm well, thank you. And you?'

He looked good. Green eyes gleaming, golden skin glowing in the apricot light of dusk, white shirt open at the neck and with the sleeves rolled back to reveal his muscular fore-arms, dark trousers cut with the spare, unforgiving elegance of English tailoring—oh, yes, he looked more than good.

Gerry felt tired and grubby.

'I'm well too,' she said courteously. She most emphati-cally did not want him inside her house again, and yet she could see that he wasn't going to go until he'd got whatever it was that had brought him there.

Sure enough, he said quietly, implacably, 'Invite me in, Geraldine.'

'Come inside, Bryn.' Her voice was flat, composed.

'Thank you.'

She led him to the kitchen and asked, 'Would you like a beer?'

'If you're having one.'

'I'll have juice.' Stooping, she picked up a bottle of Alfred's ice beer and a jug of grapefruit juice before closing the fridge door.

'Can I get down some glasses?' Bryn said.

'Unless you drink it from the bottle?' She winced as the glass bottom of the bottle rang against the stainless steel bench.

Black brows lifting, he shook his head. 'Do you?'

'No. My father had very strong ideas on how a young lady should behave—feminism passed him by completely.' She indicated a cupboard door, and as Bryn reached for two heavy-based glasses she opened the drawer and took out a bottle-opener. 'Drinking anything from the bottle was about as low as you could go and still call yourself human.'

'Let me do that,' Bryn said.

Gerry set her jaw. He certainly could; then he might not notice her shaking hands.

His were perfectly steady, as steady as his voice. 'Your father was a gentleman of the old school.'

Her heart thudded with erratic impatience; deliberately, carefully, she armoured herself against the pulsing, driving need he'd brought with him.

'Yes,' she said.

He gave her a glass and lifted his own. 'So here's to the future,' he said pleasantly, and drank.

Gerry looked away. The future. Yes, she could drink to that. 'The future,' she echoed, and took a tiny mouthful of juice. 'Come and sit down,' she urged in her most gracious, hostessy voice.

His mouth twisted slightly, but he stood back to let her lead the way to the sitting area. Once there, however, he stayed standing and surveyed the room with a long, considering gaze. 'When I walked in here the day we met,' he said, 'I thought how warm and welcoming, how serene and elegant and mischievous this room was.'

'Mischievous?' she echoed warily.

He smiled. 'It's decorated with an impeccable eye for colour and proportion but a closer look reveals the quirky things that save it from stultifying good taste. Like the glass frog on the table, and the clock.'

'It's an American acorn clock,' she said, trying to stifle the warm glow caused by his appreciation, 'about a hundred and fifty years old. I fell in love with its shape and the lovely little picture on glass, and the dealer let me pay it off by instalments, bless her.' She couldn't stop babbling. 'It was a bargain too—I got it for about half what it's worth.'

He looked at her with an enigmatic smile. 'You're nervous,' he said. 'Why?'

Gerry fought for self-possession, and managed to produce a fairly good approximation. With a faint snap in her tone she said, 'I didn't expect to see you again.'

He drank half the beer and set it down. 'I stayed away,' he said calmly, 'because I was warned that it might compromise the case if I saw you while it was in progress. And because I had a couple of things I wanted to do, and something I had to come to terms with.'

Her breath stayed locked in her chest. 'Such as?' she asked, almost dizzy with expectation too long denied.

'I had to track down the man who duped your father.'

He spoke equably, as though this was just another task ticked off.

'How did you know who he was?'

'Everyone in New Zealand knew who he was. We're too small a country for that sort of thing not to get around.'

Gerry's mouth dried. 'And did you find him?'

'In Australia, living a comfortable life in Perth.' His voice was considered, but when she stole a look at him she drew in a jagged breath at the cold glitter in his eyes.

She said, 'What happened?'

'I confronted him. He did a lot of wriggling, but in the end we came to an understanding. He agreed that you should be reimbursed, and what's left of the money is now waiting in a holding account. I know that nothing can repay you for your father's pain and death, but at least you have what is rightfully yours and the cause of it has been punished.'

'I don't believe it,' Gerry said numbly. 'How did you do it?'

His smile was sardonic. 'You don't want to know. It was legal, if a trifle unethical.'

'And will he find someone else to steal from?'

His face hardened. 'Not for some years, anyway. He's now in prison.'

She drank some of the juice, welcoming the sharp, tangy taste. 'Did you put him there?' she asked.

'I gave him a choice,' he said calmly. 'He chose what he felt was the lesser of two evils.'

She stole a careful look. 'What was the alternative?'

'Extradition to New Zealand.'

Gerry met his eyes. They were flat and deadly and opaque; he looked a very formidable man indeed. Her stomach performed a few acrobatics and she said mutedly, 'I'm very grateful.'

'You're not, you're worried, but it will be all right.' He smiled ironically. 'He didn't deserve to get away with it.'

'No, he didn't, but I don't want you doing my dirty work for me. And revenge is never a good basis for action.'

'This wasn't revenge,' he said coolly. 'It was justice.'

Still troubled, she moved to look out of the window at the new garden. Angular rust-red flowers of kangaroo paw lifted towards the sky, the spiky leaves reflected in the still, smooth water of the pool. Nosing its way slowly from beneath a waterlily leaf, the biggest and reddest of the goldfish headed across towards the other side, then gave a flick of its long white tail and disappeared into the depths.

Gerry's galloping heartbeat had eased into something like its normal speed, but she could taste the awareness on her tongue, feel Bryn's presence on her skin. Was informing her of the incarceration of her father's manager all he'd come back for? Caution clogged her tongue as she said, 'Thank you.'

'If you don't mind,' he said, 'I'd like to tell you about my sister.'

She almost held her breath. 'No, I don't mind at all.'

He looked down at his empty glass and said austerely, 'I told you that she was tall.'

'And unhappy.'

He nodded. 'Yes. It was all right while we both went to primary school, but when I was sent away to boarding school she lived for the times I came home. After I'd finished school I took an engineering degree at Christchurch, and when I came home the last time she was so thin and ill I was horrified. I took her to the doctor; he diagnosed anorexia. Apparently she'd been tormented at school about her height and her size. My grandmother was also ill, so I can't entirely blame her for not noticing what was going on.'

Gerry had guessed—of course she'd guessed—but she was horrified just the same. 'I'm so sorry,' she said, feeling wretchedly inadequate.

'I stayed with her, but it was too late. She died of heart failure.' His voice thickened. 'She was seventeen.'

She went across and wrapped his hands in both of hers. 'Oh, Bryn,' she said.

His fingers tightened on hers. 'I should have noticed.'

'How could you? You weren't there. And ten years ago people didn't know much about eating disorders.'

He let her hands go. Rebuffed, she stepped back, watching him reimpose control over his features. 'I blamed everyone—my grandparents, popular culture, the fashion magazines Anna used to pore over—but I've realised it was to hide my own guilt.'

Gerry said quietly, 'It's a normal reaction. And perhaps you were right. Our preoccupation with thinness is unhealthy.'

'I blamed you too,' he said.

'I know.'

He paused, then said deliberately, 'When I saw you with that baby in your arms I thought, Damn it all to bloody hell, there she is. My woman. It was as simple and inevitable as that, a sudden, soul-deep recognition. You were everything I thought I despised—fashionable, elegant, well-bred, beautiful, working in a career I loathed. And possibly an importer of heroin. I had to manufacture reasons for disliking you, for stopping you from affecting me, but you cut straight through into my heart and took up residence there.'

Her stomach dropped. He waited, but when she couldn't speak he said coolly, 'I soon found out that you weren't superficial and foolish; you had a natural kindness that made you take poor Lacey under your wing, and you tolerated being stranded with grace and fortitude.'

'It had to be one of the most luxurious strandings anyone's ever had,' she said huskily.

'I should have kept my distance. I'd never been at the mercy of my hormones before, but every time I saw you my gut clenched and I wanted you. I had no intention of making love to you,' he said curtly. 'I couldn't believe that you could be connected with the heroin ring, but it was a measure of how far I'd fallen in love with you that I let my passion override my common sense.' When she remained silent he added harshly, 'That had never happened to me before.'

Head bent so that he couldn't see her face, she asked, 'If you loved me, why didn't you tell me? We might not have been able to meet during the trial, but I'd have known.'

He waited so long to answer that she looked up swiftly, and saw the autocratic features set in lines of self-derision and irony. 'I was afraid to put it to the test. You gave me no indication that you wanted me for anything other than a lover.'

Gerry had lived with the knowledge of her love for so long that she couldn't believe her ears. While impetuous words clogged her tongue, he went on.

'You can't know how it felt to put you on the plane and let you go when every instinct was hammering at me to keep you with me by whatever means I had to use.'

She drew in a deep, impeded breath. The first wild delight at seeing him, at hearing him tell her what she'd only ever imagined in fantasy, was fading, leaving her fearful and tense. She asked, 'What were the other things you wanted to do?'

'I needed to see Lacey. I was determined that she wasn't going down the same road as Anna.'

'She didn't tell me,' she said in surprise.

'I asked her not to. I had to persuade her father to let her see a counsellor. She's helped, but it was your letters and your encouragement that pulled her back from the brink. She's going to be all right.'

'And the thing you had to come to terms with?'

He walked across to the French windows and stood looking out over her newly revamped garden. It had been a good summer and the plants were growing apace, lush and vigorous. On the edge of the wide deck a large pot held a tumble of petunias in soft lilacs and white and pinks.

Bryn turned away and said quietly, 'I've fought against loving anyone ever since my mother died and my father abandoned us. It hurt too much. I didn't rationalise like that, of course, when I was a kid, but I made sure I only loved Anna. And then she died. When I met you I resented what I felt for you and I was scared. Loving you—needing you—

gave you power that I was intensely reluctant to yield. It took me some time to accept that when you love someone as much as I love you, there is no capitulation. Or, if there is, it's surrender to all that's good, to a happiness I've never expected, never hoped for because I didn't think it existed. Even though I suspected you, I learned to love you. I need you, Geraldine, and I think you need me too.'

A volatile mixture of joy and dread filled her. Almost whispering, she said, 'Bryn—I must—'

Two strides brought him back to stand in front of her. For the first time, she could read what lay in the clear, glimmering depths of his eyes. Her heart turned over and agony gripped her, froze the words on her tongue, speared through her in an unrelenting torment.

With the rough note in his voice more pronounced than she'd ever heard it, he said, 'So, Geraldine, now that you're in the clear and your life's back on track, will you marry me?'

She allowed herself one radiant moment of pure, keen happiness, sharp and penetrating as a knife-blade, and then, because she didn't dare hope for more, she said, 'I'm not in the clear—I probably never will be. After the defence's insinuations plenty of people think I was in it up to my neck and managed to frame Honor. Or, if not that, that I knew what she was doing and condoned it.'

'That's stupid—'

She gave him a tight smile. 'I've been asked if I can get the stuff,' she said without bitterness.

'By whom?' There was no mistaking the lethal intentness in the quiet voice.

'It doesn't matter.'

'It matters,' he said, that menacing silky note back in his words. 'I want to know so that I can tell whoever did that they'd better back off or they'll have me to deal with.'

Gerry managed to say on a half-sob, 'It wouldn't help, Bryn. And having a wife who's been mixed up in a very unsavoury case isn't going to help your reputation.'

'If you don't want to marry me, just say so,' he said. 'Don't make excuses.'

'I don't want to marry you,' she said, listening to the sound of her heart shattering.

To her astonishment he laughed. 'Good,' he said outrageously. 'I'm going to have a wonderful time changing your mind.'

She looked at him—indomitable, tall and strong and tough—and knew that she wouldn't win. While she searched for ways to handle this—and to fight the insistent whispering from her treacherous heart that this time it might be the true, the real thing—he took her glass and raised her shaking hands to his mouth and kissed her fingertips.

In a dark, smoky voice he said, 'Marry me, Geraldine, and I'll do my utmost to make you happy, I swear it.'

'No,' she said, unshed tears burning behind her eyes. 'You don't understand, Bryn. I can't promise you that—or anything. I fall in love, but it never lasts. Eventually I get bored, or irritated, or desperate—or all three. My self-esteem takes a beating every time it happens, and you'll end up hating me. Even if you're willing to take the chance, I'm not.'

'How long does it usually last?' he demanded, not giving an inch.

She shook her head, but he lifted her chin with a hand that wouldn't be denied, and stared into her eyes as though trying to force her surrender. 'How long, damn you?'

'It's useless. I won't do this to you.'

'I won't let you go. I've been looking for you all my life and I'm not going to give up now.'

She read the truth in his eyes. Concentrated purpose blazed there, masterful, unsparing. Joy battled with terror in her heart. Summoning her utmost strength of will, she said, 'I'll be your mistress—live with you—but I won't marry you. I won't ask anything of you at all except that when I want to go you let me.' Her eyes were as hard as his; she should be sending him away, but she was racked by love, by her need for what he alone could give her.

She expected him to refuse. Bryn wasn't a man who surrendered to another's will; he'd said he was possessive, and she believed him, and the only thing she could offer him would be sheer torture for both of them.

As well as an insult.

But after staring at her for several heart-racking moments he demanded, 'What's the longest you've ever stayed in love?'

'A year,' she said, closing her eyes. 'Not more than a year.'

Silence, taut and terrifying, crackled between them. She couldn't look at him, couldn't bear the sound of her heart thudding unsteadily, painfully, in her ears.

At last he said heavily, 'All right. If that's what it takes. Only I'm setting a condition too. Two, in fact.'

'What?'

'That we don't refer to this again, and that if we're still together after two years you marry me.'

Tears roughened her voice as she said, 'All right. We'll do that.'

Gerry walked towards the front door. Yes, there he was, smiling, the green eyes lit with the secret flame that was for her and her alone, the autocratic face intent only on her.

'Good day?' he asked, shrugging off his jacket.

She smiled and reached up to kiss him briefly. 'Great. At ten o'clock this morning—just as I was driving over the Harbour Bridge—I finally got a handle on the article about computers, and I've just about finished it.'

'Of course you have,' he said.

'You must have begun to wonder, especially when you found me fretting at the laptop at three o'clock this morning,' she teased against his mouth.

'I can think of much more interesting things to do at three in the morning than obsess over an article.' His arms tightened around her and he kissed her again, his mouth demanding, seeking, a potent, heated promise.

Gerry's heart sped up. 'Mmm,' she breathed when his head lifted, 'you did. Much more interesting…'

She'd never get used to seeing him like this, eyes gleaming, all tension gone from his face.

After dropping a hard, swift kiss on her mouth, he straightened, saying, 'What are we doing tonight?'

'Nothing.' She said the word casually. Not that he'd be fooled; during the past two years he'd learned to read her most guarded tone and expression. Yet in many ways he was still an enigma to her. Oh, she understood the imperatives that drove him, and she had come to appreciate his standards and values, but although he was a tender, fierce, sensual lover, and a man she could rely on utterly, she had no idea whether he wanted to change things now that the two-year period was over.

'What are we eating?' he asked cautiously.

Laughing, she hugged him. 'I ordered in,' she said promptly. 'It'll be here in three-quarters of an hour.'

He didn't open champagne, but as she sat on the bed and talked to him while he changed from dark suit to trousers and shirt that showed off his broad shoulders and long legs so well, she told herself that she didn't care. What they had was precious enough for her; in fact, if she was any happier she might well explode with it.

The meal—prepared by one of Auckland's best restaurants—was superb, and the wine Bryn chose magnificent, a wonderful New Zealand white. At last, when they were both replete, Bryn asked, 'Brandy?'

'No, thank you.' She was curled up on the huge sofa, watching him with heavy eyes, anticipation licking feverishly through her veins. Light shimmered in a tawny aura around his head, played across the authoritative features, the arrogant nose, the strong line of jaw, the beautiful sculpture of his mouth.

He looked up and his mouth hardened. 'When you look at me like that, I want you,' he said deliberately. 'In fact, when I'm with you I'm in a constant state of arousal, but all it takes is one sleepy glance from those blue-green eyes and my body springs into violent life.'

Although his deep voice was slow and tranquil and composed, sensation sky-rocketed through her.

She smiled, and he laughed under his breath. 'Sheer magic. That smile's enough to charm the birds from heaven. I think I must be addicted to you.'

'It works both ways,' she said, aware of a faint disappointment, knowing that she had no right to be disappointed; she had set the parameters of their relationship. If he didn't want to change them she'd accept his decision, because she knew now that she loved him with a love that would last all her life.

'Addiction?' He walked across to the sofa, smiling with a set, savage movement of his mouth as she made room for him and held out her arms. Softly he said, 'Let's see if we can appease this addiction a little, shall we?'

During their time together he had introduced her to ways of making love that had thrilled and shocked her, but this time he took it very tenderly, very gently, as though she were still a virgin and this was their first time.

'It has to be addiction,' he said much later, when they were lying together, heart pressed to heart, 'because I can never get enough of you, never satisfy this need to take you. You walk ahead of me, just out of reach, too much your own woman to ever become wholly mine.'

Muscles flexed beneath skin sheened slightly with sweat as he sat up and reached for his trousers on the floor. Gerry ran an indolent finger down his spine, smiling when she felt the skin tighten beneath her fingertip. 'I am yours,' she said lazily. 'You know that.'

He smiled grimly and turned back to her. 'I know you like what you can do to me.'

From his hand dropped a shower of pearls, darkly peacock blue as a tropical lagoon at twilight, rounded and gleaming and luminous, landing on her sensitised skin with gentle impact, sliding coolly across her breasts and stomach and waist.

'Oh, darling,' she said, her voice velvet and replete, 'what on earth are these for?'

Casually pushing them aside, Bryn dropped a kiss on the slight curve of her stomach. 'It's our anniversary,' he said.

Although the vow he'd extracted from her two years ago had been uppermost in her mind for the past couple of weeks, she was filled with a quite ridiculous apprehension.

'And so?' she asked.

He scooped up a handful of pearls and spread them across her skin. 'Satin against satin. You haven't left me,' he said, not looking at her.

'No.'

'Do you want to?' His voice was level and detached, almost indifferent.

'No,' she said again, her heart pounding so heavily she thought he must be deafened by it. And because she owed him this surrender, she added jaggedly, 'Not ever.'

'In that case, I suppose the only decision we have to make is where we get married.'

Vast, consuming relief—and a strange, superstitious pang—shot through her. 'If you think,' she said forcefully, 'that that is any sort of proposal, you'd better think again.'

'Do you want me to go down on my knees?' His mouth was taut, and still he wouldn't look at her. 'I will if you want me to. You know that I'd do anything to keep you, anything at all.'

She wound her arms around him, pulling his lean, naked body down to her. 'All you need to do is say that you forgive me for thinking that what I feel for you was anything like the way I felt for any other man,' she said unevenly. 'These past two years have been the happiest in my life. I don't ever want to leave you—sometimes I wake up in the middle of the night terrified that it's all been a dream, that you don't love me, that I drove you away because I was stupid enough to think that I was like my mother. And I stare into an empty world, dark and hopeless.'

His mouth touched her trembling one, stifling the fever-ish words.

'Hush,' he murmured, 'there's nothing to forgive. Nothing. I love you, and I'd follow you to the ends of the earth, give you anything you ever asked for, even if it was a life together with no formal ties.'

'I was frightened when I made that stipulation,' she admitted.

'I know. But I was almost convinced that you loved me. I have no idea what drove your mother, but you're not like her. Along with the passion and the fire and that keen, astute brain, you're sane and kind and loving—all I'll ever want. And I knew it the moment I walked into the kitchen in the villa and saw you cuddling that baby—even though I still thought you were mixed up with the drug ring.'

'The sight of me holding a baby convinced you I wasn't?' she asked, running her fingertips over the smooth swell of his shoulder.

'Yes. Even though I knew of that trail to Switzerland, neatly labelled with your name. You were so concerned about the child. It didn't jell with Geraldine the smart, so-phisticated woman of the world, or Geraldine the drug smuggler. But it wasn't faked. After that, although I strug-gled hard to keep an unbiased mind, in my heart I knew you couldn't have done it, because you valued life too much to be caught up in a filthy trade like that.'

She kissed the side of his throat and said, 'Maddie's all right now. I had lunch with her today.'

'Good.' But he spoke absently. His mouth touched a cer-tain spot below her ear and she shivered. 'Speaking of ba-bies,' he said huskily, 'how do you think I'd be as a father?'

She smiled dreamily. 'You'll be a wonderful father,' she whispered. 'But we'd better get married first because chil-dren need stability. They need to know that their parents are going to be there for them. They need to know that their parents care enough about each other to get married.'

Although they'd decided on a small wedding, somehow it turned into a huge one, a riotous affair with cousins and children and friends mingling in a day-long summer celebration. Afterwards they went to Longopai, their honeymoon interrupted only by a visit to the atoll where they'd first made love, and first known that they loved.

It was there, lying in the shade of the palms, that Bryn said, 'By the way, I've found the baby.'

'What?'

He opened a sleepy eye and smiled into her puzzled face. 'The abandoned baby. The one you found outside your house.'

Against his chest she asked, 'How did you find her? The social welfare wouldn't tell you.'

'I sent someone to dig deep. She's been adopted. Would you like to see her?'

'Could I?'

'We wouldn't be able to tell them who we are. And I think it should only be the once.'

She nodded. 'Yes, they have their lives,' she said slowly, reluctantly. Then she smiled. They hadn't used any precautions at all since the wedding. With any luck she might be pregnant herself.

A month later she walked across the crisp green grass of the Domain in Auckland towards a hillside seething with excited children and parents. A cool wind blew, but the children in their vivid clothes lit up the glowing green hillside as vividly as the array of kites.

'Over there,' Bryn said, nodding at a couple. The woman, young and slightly overweight, bent to tie up the laces of a child, while a thin young man looked up from a kite laid out on the ground and said something that made both mother and daughter laugh.

Gerry looked at the child. Chubby, rosy in the crisp air, she had candy-floss hair and big blue eyes. Her mother straightened the hood of her anorak, and picked her up. The child snuggled against her mother's shoulder, and both watched as her father lifted the kite and began to run with it. The gusting wind caught it, snatched it and tossed it high into the sky on the end of its string.

The child laughed and clapped her hands, and her mother smiled at her. Another facet of love, Gerry thought.

Quietly she said, 'Goodbye,' and added as mother and daughter followed the man and the kite, 'I didn't even realise that I needed to see her—just to make sure.' She raised a radiant face and said, 'You know me better than I do myself.'

Bryn hugged her and turned her around, walking her back to the car. 'Underneath that elegant mask you're as soft as butter,' he teased.

'So are you.'

He laughed. 'Where you're concerned, yes. But then, why wouldn't I be? You make my life complete.'

'Not just me,' she said demurely. 'I hope not, anyway, because in eight months' time there's going to be another of us.'

His arm tightened around her. When she looked up she saw the sudden intense glitter of tears in his eyes, and then he said, 'Geraldine.'

In that word, said with such raw need, such tenderness, she heard everything she'd ever want to hear. Hand in hand, they walked down the hill and into their future.

Harlequin Romance®

Delightful

Affectionate

Romantic

Emotional

Tender

Original

Daring

Riveting

Enchanting

Adventurous

Moving

Harlequin Romance—the
series that has it all!

HROM-G

◆ Harlequin®
◆ Historical

From rugged lawmen and
valiant knights to defiant heiresses
and spirited frontierswomen,
Harlequin Historicals will
capture your imagination with
their dramatic scope, passion
and adventure.

Harlequin Historicals…
they're too good to miss!

HHGENR

HARLEQUIN®

I N T R I G U E®

We'll leave you breathless!

If you've been looking for thrilling tales of
contemporary passion and sensuous love stories
with taut, edge-of-the-seat suspense—
then you'll *love* **Harlequin Intrigue!**

Every month, you'll meet four new heroes
who are guaranteed to make your spine tingle
and your pulse pound. With them you'll enter
into the exciting world of Harlequin Intrigue—
where your life is on the line
and so is your heart!

THAT'S INTRIGUE—DYNAMIC ROMANCE AT ITS BEST!

HARLEQUIN®

I N T R I G U E®

INT-GENR

HARLEQUIN® AMERICAN ROMANCE®

LOOK FOR OUR FOUR FABULOUS MEN!

Each month some of today's bestselling authors bring
four new fabulous men to Harlequin American Romance.
Whether they're rebel ranchers, millionaire power brokers
or sexy single dads, they're all gallant princes—and
they're all ready to sweep you into lighthearted fantasies
and contemporary fairy tales where anything is possible
and where all your dreams come true!

You don't even have to make a wish...
Harlequin American Romance will grant your every desire!

Look for Harlequin American Romance
wherever Harlequin books are sold!

HAR-GEN

HARLEQUIN SUPERROMANCE®

...there's more to the story!

Superromance. A *big* satisfying read about unforget-
table characters. Each month we offer
four very different stories that range from family
drama to adventure and mystery, from highly emo-
tional stories to romantic comedies—and
much more! Stories about people you'll
believe in and care about. Stories too
compelling to put down....

Our authors are among today's *best* romance writers. You'll find familiar names and
talented newcomers. Many of them are
award winners—and you'll see why!

If you want the biggest and best
in romance fiction, you'll get it
from Superromance!

Available wherever Harlequin books are sold.

Look us up on-line at: http://www.romance.net

HS-GEN